Seven

A Novel By

~ Diamond Cartel ~

This book is a work of fiction. Any characters, incidents, situations, or the like are not real nor are they based on actual events. Similarities to individuals, living or deceased, are purely coincidental and not deliberately intentional.

Seven © 2019 by Diamond Cartel. All Rights Reserved. Printed in the United States of America. No part of this book may be copied, duplicated, reprinted, or reproduced in any form (print, digital, verbal, or otherwise) under any circumstances without written consent from the author.

ISBN: 978-0-578-51205-1

Isys Publications, LLC
Columbus, Ohio 43211
www.isysconnections.com

There is no greater sin than that of self destruction.

Acknowledgements

So much has happened between my last release, Sisterly Bond, and this book. My creativity has changed. My beliefs have changed. My circle has changed. One thing that has stayed the same is my love, adoration, and dependency on God. Without my Higher Power there is no way I would still be here.

Family means everything to me. Whether I was born in it, bred from it, or became part of it, I appreciate you all.

My tribe is just as important as my family. I have several and thank God every day for sending such amazing beings of light, love, and highest vibrational energy into my life.

In conclusion, I'd like to thank you – the reader – for your love and support. Whether this is your first time hearing of me, or you've been rocking with me since Hurricane, your support is what keeps me going. Thank you for your presence in this journey.

Take care and enjoy!

Expressively yours,

Diamond Cartel

Wren

I can't believe it's come down to this. A few months ago, my life was nearly perfect. I had a wonderful job, a loving fiancé, and great friends. Everything was going well. All that changed in a matter of hours. Now, I'm surrounded by police, SWAT, helicopters, and flashing lights. It's hotter than Hades up in here. As I stand here with this smoking gun in my hand, surrounded by bodies, I start to drift off to a past where life was so much simpler.

"Wren, I need to see you in my office immediately!"

Mr. Warren only had that tone of voice with me under two circumstances; when he was under a strenuous deadline or when he felt like we were going to lose a case. Seeing as I was part of the legal team defending a seven-time serial rapist, I felt it was the latter. I jumped up and rushed to his office. When he closed the door, I knew it was serious.

I spent the next two hours stuck in his office with James, my partner on this case. As we got our asses chewed out, all I could think of was the quickest way to either get our client off the hook or take a plea deal at the very least. We've been working on this case for almost three years and we are still no closer to finding him innocent or guilty than we were on day one. The entire situation was getting old to me. My patience was out the window.

At the end of the meeting Mr. Warren told us to do what we had to do to save our client. Not that this was a high profile case or anything; he just wanted to free up our time so we could start working on our next case – his daughter's vehicular homicide charge. That was another nightmare I was not ready to deal with; out one shit hole just to be put in another.

By the end of the day, I was spent. The only thing I wanted to do was to go home, take a hot shower and cuddle up with my honey, Jason. He is the only one that can bring my tension down after a day like this. A nice back rub, a few shots of Henny, and some good sex were all I needed to get back on my A-game.

On my way home I called my best friend, Laila. It was routine for us to call each other after work to whine and bitch about our day. Sadly, that was how most of our conversations went. Very rarely did we have anything positive to say about work; then again, who does?

Talking with her always made my hour and a half commute from Atlanta to Marietta somewhat easier. It's only a twenty minute drive, but with traffic and these non-driving mother fuckers down here I'm lucky to do it in that time frame. I love Atlanta to pieces, but I'm really considering a location change. As usual, my traffic frustrations were part of our conversation.

"Seriously?!" I yell at the black Durango that just cut me off. "Learn how to fuckin' drive!"

Laila laughs at me on the other end, just before letting out her own outburst.

"Girl, I don't know how you deal with that drive every day." She said. "I'm only going down Peachtree and I'm ready to slap somebody!"

"I don't have a choice, but after the way Mr. Warren chewed me up and spit me out today, I might not have to worry about this commute much longer."

I wasn't concerned about losing my job as much as I was about losing my sanity over this damn case.

"Don't stress it, Wren-nnn."

She said my name with the fry. You know, that extended last syllable. That could mean only one thing.

"Who do you see? How fine is he? And how long before you hit?"

"Caramel, eight out of ten, and two days tops!"
"You're such a hoe!"
"Bitch, please! This hoe has needs, and he is about to fulfill every one of them."

Let me back up for a second. Laila, as much as I love her, has a severe sexual addiction. She's the type of female that I'd keep my man ten thousand feet from if I had any worries. Luckily, she respects our 14-year friendship enough not to even look sideways at Jason. Not to mention early in our friendship I had to show her how not to cross me when it comes to my man. She tried that shit once with my college boyfriend. All it took was a busted eye and broken arm. I haven't had any issues out of her since.

Fast forward to now, she's still hot in the pants and has a sex drive that I will probably never be able to understand. Jason and I are known to get it in about five times a week. She calls us the eighty-year-old couple. Apparently, what we do in a week is what she does in a day – if the guy and conditions are right.

"Focus, Laila."
"I will in a few seconds."

While on hold, I could hear her running her usual game; stroking this unknown man's ego in ways that no man could resist. Then I hear clicks…she must be entering his number. Laila never gives her number out; she's a bit of a control freak. I feel her on that end. Some of these thirsty dudes get desperate. After a few moments she gets back on the phone.

"Okay, I'm back."
"You sure about that?"
"Shut up!"
"Sometimes you amaze me with the things you do." I said, laughing.

"I tend to have that effect on people. So, what are you going to do about your case?"

"I'm going to let James stress over it tonight. I, on the other hand, am about to go home and get spoiled to death."

"Aww!"

"Shut it!"

"Whatever. I'm about to set my plan in motion so I can unwrap my eye candy."

"Have fun with that. I'll hit you up later."

"Oh, you bet I will!"

When I pulled into the driveway my stress level decreased dramatically. There is a rule between Jason and I that whatever happens in the outside world stays there. Our home is a place just for us and negative energy is not allowed in our space. I stepped out of my Lexus RX350, exhaled everything I felt in that moment, and prepared to step into paradise.

"Welcome home, babe." Jason greeted me with the most passionate kiss at the door. He took my briefcase and purse from me and placed it by the coat rack at the door. Motioning for me to turn around, I slid my coat off for him to hang up.

"Thanks, baby." I said, showing off my dimple he loved so much.

"No thanks needed. Your only job tonight is to relax and let me take care of you."

We went over to the sofa and he sat me down on the couch. I stretched out and placed my feet on his lap. No words passed my lips as I slipped into pampered paradise. Jason truly treated me like a queen, and I loved every second of it.

Jason is what most women would consider God in physical manifestation. He's 6'5", athletically built - not big, but muscular. Granted he's not wealthy, but he does make a nice six figure salary. Everything that most women are looking for, he's got. Even the emotions they're seeking – the care, adoration, attention, passion – he gives to me freely and unreservedly. He never fails to make me feel like I'm the only woman in existence.

I must have drifted off because I woke up to the smell of my favorite dinner – fettuccini alfredo with chicken, broccoli, and mozzarella cheese, homemade garlic bread, and cannoli topped with vanilla bean ice cream and caramel sauce. God bless him and his Italian genes from his mother's side. Next to his five-cheese turkey lasagna, this is one of his specialties.

Dinner was amazing as always. I was ready for dessert, and I'm not referring to the cannoli he made…although I could think of a few things we could do with them. Jason must have had the same thought because they were brought with us as we headed back to the room.

"How are you feeling, my little songbird?"

He always calls me that, partly because of my name and partly because of my incessant desire to sing. No matter what mood I'm in I always find myself belting out a tone. According to others I have an amazing voice, one that is rarely found these days, but singing is just not my forte. It's more of a mood indicator than anything else. You can always tell what I'm feeling based on the song I'm singing.

"I'm a lot better than I was a few hours ago."

He placed his finger to my lips.

"Let's not talk about that. Right now, in this moment, it's all about you. I want you to be totally relaxed and ready for what's about to happen."

Laid out on our California king-sized bed he slowly began to peel off my clothes. Not in a sexual way, but more sensual. I knew this moment wasn't about him getting ready to fuck me. This was our routine when we needed to release stress. There was a special method we used on each other to release endorphins that naturally relieved our anxiety and anger.

With nothing but sheer anticipation covering my frame, the lights went off and candles were lit throughout the room. The scent of chamomile filled the room while light jazz played in the background. With every passing second, I was drifting farther away from reality and into a world of complete bliss and serenity.

Jason had done it again. In fifteen minutes, I went from ready to execute the next person that spoke to utter tranquility. I would be in this space for however long necessary to reset my energy centers as Jason would explain it. I must admit when he first did this for me, I thought he was one of those eccentric spiritual gurus or something, but it worked. It has been my stress relief medicine ever since.

I was in Zen for over two hours, but it felt longer. As I regained consciousness, I could feel my heart beating a soft, rhythmic melody – I started harmonizing with it. A simple smile spread across my face and tears began to stream from my eyes. This was quite alarming when I first had this experience. Now it is welcomed and embraced. Without this practice I'm sure I would have caught quite a few cases of my own by now.

I didn't move right away. Jason always says it's best to take your time when coming out of intense relaxation. It took me close to twenty minutes to readjust to my surroundings and gain enough strength to move my body. These moments always seem to last forever and simultaneously be over in an instant.

When I walked out to the living room I could hear Jason getting off the phone.

"Hey, baby." He greeted me with a kiss. "Feeling better?"

"So much better! Thank you for taking such good care of me."

"That's what I'm here for. Now that I got you mentally straight let's work on the physical."

Jason is such a passionate romantic. He loves to please me in every sense of the word. I don't know what I've done to be so lucky, but I'm beyond grateful that he's mine. We've been together for so long that I honestly don't remember much about my life before he came into the picture. Twenty years is a long time to know someone. It's also long enough to know they're in your life beyond a reason or a season.

From the moment his lips brushed against my neck, and his warm and soft breath comforted me in its gentle breeze, I was instantly in heaven. With Jason, sex wasn't just sex – it was an experience; a creation of sorts that only he could produce, direct, and be the starring actor. And here I am, his leading lady; ready, willing, and able to do anything and everything he asks me to do.

That's just what I did for the next two hours. I was bent, stretched, whipped, caressed, sucked, fucked, rubbed down, *dicked* down…you name it, we did it. The air was thick and hot from our lovemaking. In the end, we both climaxed to a new height, sending our limp, lifeless, yet satisfied bodies crashing to the floor on top of our Persian rug.

He held me in his arms, and like a child, I wept. How is it that I am so deserving of such intense passion? How is it that after all these years, no matter how much I yelled, screamed, or attacked him he was still willing to give me the best of him every time? Even in my moments of rage he still holds me down. I can be a handful at times, but he handles me perfectly.

The next day I was refreshed, renewed, and ready to take on anything that came my way. Not only did I feel good, it was Friday and it was lady's night with the girls. We tried to get together at least every other month because we all have such busy schedules. But those schedules keep the money flowing our way and I have yet to hear any of the ladies complaining. Well, except for Nelli, but we'll get to her later.

The moment I stepped into the office I was called into the conference room. Mr. Warren was already in there with James and our client. Apparently, someone forgot to mention this impromptu meeting to me. I walked in and everyone was semi-happy. It scared the hell out of me.

"Hello, Mr. Larsen." I said to our client. "How are you doing today?"

"A lot better now that I know I have a great defense team."

I looked over at James and before his lips could part Mr. Warren filled me in on everything that was going on. According to Mr. Warren, there were a few discrepancies on how evidence was collected from the crime scene. Mr. Larsen is the primary suspect in the murder of a 17-year-old girl. He has no connection to her, but he was somehow linked to the house where her body was found naked and decomposing in a trunk. I personally felt he was guilty, but my job is to keep them out of jail, not put them in it. Sometimes I really questioned if I was on the right side of the law. Then again, I already knew the answer.

"Wow, that's great news." I said as enthusiastically as possible. "Has this information been presented to the other side?"

"Not yet." James said. "We got a heads up from a rookie reporter. They obviously don't teach discretion in communications class."

"So how do you know this reporter's claims are accurate?" My skepticism grew.

The more they talked the more it started to look like they were grabbing on to any piece of hope they could to appease Mr. Larsen. I knew at that point his case was a lost cause, yet it is my job as his attorney to give him all the hope he can muster…so I went along with the program.

"That sounds great! We can win this case after all." I heard the biggest laugh in the back of my head, but I ignored it and continued. "Now all we need to do is present this evidence to the judge. This is as close to an open and shut case as we're going to get."

"Sounds good to me." Mr. Warren said. "See, Mr. Larsen? You're in good hands."

The cocky expression that overtook his face instantly disgusted me. Not that it mattered. He was on the fast track to rotting in the nearest jail cell. Unfortunately, he's a pretty boy too. He was about to become someone's bitch.

Laila

"I'll call you tomorrow, baby." I said, as I watched the black Lexus pull out of my driveway.

That was Andre; yet another notch in my belt. I had no intention of ever calling or speaking to him again. I never do. Men are disposable to me. They give me anything I want, without even asking for it; take me on exotic vacations; pamper me like the princess that I am. They give me the world without a single request from me. All I need to do is swing my naturally curly, auburn hair, bat my light brown eyes, and position my statuesque body in a way where no curve goes unnoticed - and voila, they are putty at my feet!

It's become so second nature that the thrill of it is gone. Now I find excitement in watching them compete. One male suitor will see me with a new diamond bracelet and, without even asking if I bought it for myself, will take it upon himself to buy a matching necklace and earrings. Another will see me in a new pair of Jimmy Choo's or Louboutin's and buy me a complete outfit to go with it, then request that I wear it on a night in the town. I don't see how women can complain there are so many broke, lazy, worthless men in the world. I seem to attract the opposite all the time.

I guess my looks could have something to do with it. It's not every day you see a perfectly blended Asian, Hawaiian, and African American chick with thick, long, curly hair, a 38D-26-40 figure, and not a scar, scratch, or stretch mark on me. Not bad for a 5'4" cutie pie if I do say so myself. It could be that. Or it could be my magnetizing energy that drives men to do insane things just to catch my attention. Or it could be that I am the daughter of the wealthiest and most trusted chief of surgery in the city of Atlanta.

I have to name things outside of sex because that's not what lures these men to me...but it is what makes it hard for them to leave. I don't sleep with everyone who gives me gifts.

Only a select few can cross the threshold to my bedroom. But once they do it is guaranteed they will never leave my room the same way they came in.

The latest - and so far, greatest - to have entered my world is Malcolm. I met him last week at Gainell's housewarming party. Her twin, Giuseppina, introduced me to him. She said he seemed like he was my type, and damn it if she wasn't right. Malcolm was tall, built like a football player, rich, and had the sex drive of a rabbit. He's everything I want in a man, but there is still something missing. There always is.

My highly driven sex life didn't start off voluntarily. My stepfather Nate, now deceased, started it for me. While the incident only happened once, I still can't shake the fact that he took my virginity without my permission. He was high and I was scared; it made for a cesspool of destruction. He penetrated me repeatedly until he finally came inside of me. He didn't even bother to pull out. It only lasted five minutes, but it seemed like an eternity. He rolled off me, stumbled down the hall, and passed out on the couch. I immediately took a shower and scrubbed the dirty feeling off me. An hour later, my mother came home, saw him on the couch, and woke him up to go to bed.

A month later, my period was missing in action. I began to panic, but I didn't say anything. My mother kept asking me questions because she hadn't seen any tampon wrappers in the bathroom. She started accusing me of having sex with guys - I didn't even have a boyfriend yet. Nate was beginning to panic as well. He knew something happened that night, but he was so high on weed and prescription drugs that his memory was vague. When my mother mentioned to him that she thought I was having sex it triggered something in him. It was all finally coming back to him, and neither one of us liked where it was going.

My best friend at the time, Gina, took me to get a pregnancy test. I took the test at her house while her parents were at work. In two minutes my biggest fear was realized. I was pregnant. I went from being a virgin, not giving a damn about boys or sex, to being pregnant by my stepfather all within three weeks! Who does that? Apparently, I do.

This was not about to happen. I had to do something, but I was underage and couldn't get an abortion without parental consent. If I told my mom what happened she would kill us both. Even if I didn't say anything it would eventually come out; I could only hide a pregnancy for so long. I didn't know what to do, but something had to be done quick.

One night, when my mom was at work, Nate came into my room. Instantly, my guard went up.

"If you touch me again I swear this lamp will go upside your head!" I said in immediate defense.

"Stop, Laila. I have a solution, but you're going to have to trust me."

I knew something was up. I could sense he had the same fear that I did, but I didn't care. This mother fucker violated me in the ultimate way, and now he wants me to trust him? This must be a joke. But given the situation I didn't have much of a choice. With the lamp gripped tightly in my hand, I listened to what he had to say.

His plan made sense, but it was fucked up all the same. If I followed through, he would, once again, be screwing me repeatedly. Now, not only did he take my virginity, but he was about to be the cause of me losing my first child. At that moment I wanted him to rot in the deepest, darkest, hottest part of hell the devil could find. But he wasn't there yet - I was.

"Fine. I'll do it."

With that said, he walked away from my door. Two weeks later he signed for me to have an abortion. That incident was never brought up again. My mother never found out. It would be a secret we'd both take to the grave. He just so happened to take it sooner than I anticipated.

I was sixteen when that happened. Ever since he took me to get an abortion he was putty in my hands. It didn't matter what I asked for, did, or wanted, he found a way to make it happen. I discovered that I had some sort of power over him. He felt guilty for what he did to me. That kind of power turned me on. It wasn't until his death five years ago from a car accident that I realized what kind of control I really had. But when he died, so did that power. I missed it and was determined to get it back.

I guess that's how I ended up the way I am now. Something about sexual domination turned me on. It wasn't the sex directly - half the time the guys sucked. Yet the control I had over men gave me a rush. I needed that in my life. When Nate was alive, I had it. My mom thought we just finally decided to bond and was happy he went above and beyond for me. I'm an only child so it didn't seem weird or out of sorts to her. When he died, she was devastated and so was I, but for a different reason.

But I digress. When it comes to Malcolm, he reminds me of Nate. In fact, all my past men remind me of him. My mom makes this joke about how my boyfriends emulated Nate. Sometimes she even goes as far as to say I must have had a crush on him. Her innocence of the situation is adorable and heartbreaking at the same time. I want to tell her the truth, I really do, but what good would it do now? He's dead. I'm an adult. She's moved on and recently remarried. The damage is done. They say let sleeping dog lie, and that's exactly what I plan to do for the rest of my life.

My condo reeked of sex. It's a pheromone during the act, but afterwards it just turns my stomach. I opened the windows to let in some fresh air - and let out the funk - and changed my sheets. After tiding up a bit I called my friend Phoenix to meet up for a shopping date. Malcolm threw me a couple stacks before he left, so I decided to spread the wealth. My girls have been there for me through thick and thin so when given the opportunity I always spoil them. There were plenty of times when I couldn't and they did the same for me. It's just how we roll. She was down so we agreed to meet up in a couple of hours. That gave me time to shower, get dressed, and check in with my mom.

    Phoenix and I met up at Westridge Shopping Center. It's been a couple of weeks since we've seen each other. It was good to have some quality time with one of my best friends. We spent hours in the mall, went out to dinner, and then grabbed a movie. These moments are few and far in-between for us, but they're always a blast.

    At the end of the night we got the girls together at her house for an impromptu lady's night. We were all sitting in Phoenix's grand living room: Gainell (Nelli), her twin Giuseppina (GiGi), Wren, Emerald (Emma), Summer, and myself; catching up on old times, cracking up on new times, and fueling each other's fire for something more. These were the moments I lived for with the women I'd die for. At this very moment life was good. Who could ask for anything more?

Phoenix

After the week I had, it felt good to spend some quality time with my girls. They would ride or die for me if I needed them to. If Darrin doesn't get his act together it just may come to that. Darrin and I have been having some problems - to be clear, his hand has a problem with my face. The first couple of times I handled it myself. Once it went from being an open hand to a closed fist, things changed.

That's not the focus tonight. I just need some positive energy in my life. Something fun, fresh, and free - like spending time with my girls. It was especially nice to hang out with Laila again. I forgot how much debauchery we cause when we're together. It was well worth it; she's still as feisty and fearless as ever. I used to be like that. In some ways I know it's still in me. I should get rid of this abnormal growth called a boyfriend. I'm too old to have one of those anyway.

"What are you daydreaming about over there, Phoe?" GiGi asked tossing a pillow at my head.

"Nothing, heifer, and quit throwing my pillows around before you knock something over!"

"Then answer my question."

"What question?"

"What happened between you and old' girl in your marketing class?"

"Dana? I put that bitch in her place, what else?"

"You're bad!" Emma said.

"No, I just know she crossed the line and I had to push her back a few paces."

"That's my girl!" Laila said giving me a high five.

There was always some shit going on in my life. If it wasn't Darrin it was school. If it wasn't that it was family drama. If it wasn't that then I was going to bat for one of my girls. My life is a constant war with no time to rest in between battles. I am tired, drained, and tapped out. If something didn't give soon it would be my sanity. If that leaves then I feel sorry for anyone around me.

"All I know is that I've had it up to here with the bullshit." I said waving my hand over my head.

"All the more reason you need to cut all of these sorry mother fuckers off!" Wren jumped in. She was the feisty one. If anyone could feel my anguish it would be her.

"I know, Wren, but it's hard. Shit is always coming at me."

"Because you let it!" Now Laila was laying into me. "Sometimes, Phoe, you have to say fuck everyone else and look out for yourself. How many of these people you're stressing over would give their last and lay down their life for you? Can you name one?"

"Well…" I started. She knew what I was going to say.

"…and I'm not talking about us! Unless we're stressing you."

"No, you guys are my stress relievers."

Damn it, I was beginning to get emotional. They could sense it, too. Emma wasn't one for emotions, so she changed the subject quickly. It wasn't because she couldn't handle them; she just preferred to only talk about things that had to deal with her.

"Enough with this mushy shit! Have y'all seen Diane's new car?" She abruptly interrupted. "How in the hell is she able to afford that?"

"Jealous, much?" Nelli said, jokingly.

"Me? Of what? Her car is just as tacky as she is."

"But isn't that the same SUV you had our eye on? And the same color?" Wren pointed out.

Emma started to stare her down, but knew not to cross that line with her. Before another word could be spoken Summer broke it up.

"Hey, y'all, just chill!" Summer had a way of being real stern with her soft, relaxed tone. "We're supposed to be vibing, not fighting."

"Summer's right." I said. "This is not the time or place for any more unnecessary drama."

"My bad." Emma said, cleaning it up. "You're right. It's not that serious."

"It never is." Laila chimed in. "So, back to vibing we go."

The rest of the night we talked, drank, danced, and laughed until one by one we passed out. By three in the morning we were all dead to the world. It was the first peaceful night's sleep I've had in a few months. I really needed this; more than I led on.

The next morning, I was the last one to wake up. It was close to noon by the time I rolled off the sofa bed. Laila, Wren, and Summer were all over my house cleaning up. The other girls had helped but left before I got up. I stumbled into the kitchen just as Laila closed the fridge door.

"Good morning, sleepy head!" She said, giving me a hug. "Well, afternoon."

"Why did you guys let me sleep so long?"

"Because we knew you needed it. Look, I get that you don't want to go into details about what's going on with you, and that's fine, but just know you don't have to go through it alone, okay?"

She grabbed my arms. I stood in front of her trying to be strong and not cry my eyes out. It was hard, but I managed to keep it together.

"I know. You're all the best." We hugged.

"GiGi and Nelli cleaned up your basement and Emma took care of your room upstairs before they had to leave. Wren is outside beating something to oblivion, your rug, I think. Summer and I just came back from the store. We filled your fridge with that healthy crap you love so much."

"You girls are too much!"

"Anything for our sister!"

Wren walked back in the house with one of my throw rugs. She looked like she just released some of her own pinned up anger.

"Are you okay, Wren?" I asked her.

"Girl I'm good." She replied. "Stinky, sweaty, but good." She took a whiff of herself. "And on that note, I got to go. I need a serious shower."

"Thanks for beating my rug."

"Please don't say it like that. I don't swing that way."

I started to laugh.

"I didn't mean it like that! Nasty heifer!"

"I'm just saying."

Wren got her things together and left a few minutes later. Summer wasn't too far behind her. Within fifteen minutes of me waking up, it was just me and Laila.

"What do you have going on today?" Laila asked.

"I'm not sure, but I hope it doesn't involve any drama."

"It doesn't have to involve any if you don't want it around."

"I wish it was that simple, Laila. If it were, I wouldn't have slept until noon today."

"Do you want to talk about it now since everyone's gone?"

"Nah. I'm good."

"No, you're not, but I'll let you slide…for now."

"Damn you for knowing me so well."

"That's why I hold the title of best friend, hoochie!"

"Hoochie? Who in the hell still says that?!"

"Leftover liquor; leave me alone!"

We both laughed. Laila hung out with me until it was time for her to get ready for work. The extra couple hours did me good. After she left, I was at the house alone.

"Well, Phoenix, what are you going to do now?"

Go to sleep.

I looked around, expecting to see Laila pop up from behind the couch playing a prank.

Go to sleep.

There it is again. I walked to the front and back doors and they were both locked. No one was in the house except for me. Clearly, I was still tired; maybe I do need to go to sleep.

Go to sleep.

I remembered what my girls said. Sometimes you need to shut everyone out and take time for yourself. Without a second thought I turned my phone off, headed to my bedroom, closed the curtains and passed out for another six hours.

Emerald

"That bitch always has drama going on." I tried to explain my frustration to GiGi, but she just wasn't getting it.

"Emma, leave Phoenix alone. You know she's been going through it these past few months. Why do you insist on giving her such a hard time?"

I guess she had a point, but Phoenix has everything laid out for her. She owns her home and car, has a cushiony, six figure job, her man is fine as hell, and she's child free. What else does she want? Here I am stuck in this one bedroom apartment, my car is on its last wheel, I'm working a dead end job, and I'm constantly attracting lame ass dudes. If anyone has the right to complain it's me, but I don't. Who is she to bitch and moan because her dude is too protective, or her job is too stressful?

"That's just it. She doesn't have to deal with any of it. I don't understand people who complain about shit they can fix, but they don't."

"It's her situation and you have no place or say so to judge it."

"Maybe not, but I also don't have to listen to it neither."

"Then don't."

"Excuse me?"

"Don't listen to it. Tell her that you wish her the best, but there's not much you can do, and since you're pretty much useless in helping with a solution you'd rather not listen to it."

"What do you mean I'm pretty much useless?"

"Emma, you just said it yourself that you don't want to hear it. You think the simple solution is to just leave behind what bothers her. Obviously, your solution wouldn't work for her. That's the only thing you've suggested, so unless you have something else you might as well say your suggestions are pretty much useless."

I sat in silence, not because I was surprised, but because GiGi was right. GiGi always had a way with getting her point across. I guess that's why we were closer than everyone else. We're like two sides of the same coin. I want it all, she has it all. In some ways I live vicariously through her. It curbs my urge to do certain things to get what I want. The difference between us is that while I'm stuck at the desire stage, she can obtain anything she wants.

"You know I can't stand when you're right."

"It's not about being right. It's about looking out for our friend. You two aren't vibing about the situation right now, but you must remember that it's her situation, not yours. There's very little you can say to her about how to handle it. If you can't be there as a supportive friend then remove yourself altogether."

"Damn, you make me sound like the worst friend in the world."

"No, not like that. You know your limitations, which is good, but you also need to know your place as her friend. That's all I'm saying."

"Yeah, I got you."

"I got to go. Nelli and I are going to our parent's house. I'll talk to you later."

"Alright, girlie. Thanks for talking some sense to me."

"That's why I'm here."

I hung up the phone still reeling from Phoenix's so-called drama. As much as I tried to listen to what GiGi was saying, my ego simply wasn't with it. When this feeling comes over me, I know it's time to hit the gym. If I don't then I'm at jeopardy of saying or doing something that I usually regret later. I got in my car and headed out to put my feelings to work.

The gym was unusually packed. I hadn't seen this many people here since the beginning of the year. They must be running a special or something. Whatever; so long as there was a treadmill available. They can do whatever they want, but I needed to run. I walked upstairs to the cardio room and fuck me in the ass if there wasn't one single treadmill available. I just went from irritated to straight up angry.

    I had to settle for the elliptical even though I hated that machine. It's too hard for my petite figure; I had to jump up to even get on the machine. I'll bear it until someone stops running. Then I'll switch and I dare someone to cut in front of me.

    For almost an hour I struggled, but I must admit by the time a treadmill became available I was no longer wangry. Maybe the stair climber wasn't so bad after all. I still made the switch just so I could get in my run. The irritation had evaporated. Phoenix really had a way of getting to me. The other girls had their moments, too, but that girl right there makes me want to wring her damn neck! I try to keep my composure when she gets in her moods, but sometimes I step back for a week or two. You know, to keep myself from committing a 187.

    My workout routine is insane. I'm here at this gym seven days a week for at least three hours every day and I still don't see my desired figure. I'm not really that tall, only about 5'5", but for my height I should not weight 130 pounds. That's too damn much and I have nothing to show for it; no ass, no tits, nothing! Then you got these skinny bitches coming up in here like they need to work out. It's all good though because when I get right they'll all be hating. Every single one of these birds will know about me.

Wren

"Yo, Wren!"

What does this fool want now? I went downstairs to see Jason sitting in the living room with his best friends Walter and Cameron. When those three get together it's nothing but trouble. I already feel like shit warmed over. The last thing I need is for them to start messing with me.

"What, Jay?"

"Come here, baby. I miss you."

"You do realize it's too early to be gone, right?!"

His friends started laughing, but I was serious. Usually I find Jason's antics cute. Today I just want to stay in bed and sleep through whatever this icky feeling that's taken over me.

"What's wrong with you?" He said half-heartedly.

Immediately my eyes started watering and I felt like I was about to collapse on the stairs.

"I can't do this with you right now." I said as I turned to go back to bed.

I went up the stairs and he was right on my heels. By the time I made it back to my room I became dizzy and fainted. Luckily, he was there to catch me and lay me down.

"Babe, you are burning up! Do you need to go to the doctor?"

"No." I said matter-of-factly. "I'll be fine. Just let me go back to sleep."

"Are you sure?"

I growled at him. Literally, I made a sound that would have sent a bear into hiding. Anyone who knows me well knows not to aggravate me when I'm sick. Jason could usually get away with it. He's good at getting me to do things I don't want to do if he knows it will be good for me. But today was not his day.

I must have scared him off because he left the room and didn't say another word to me. I heard some mumbling downstairs and then the door shut. I don't know if he left or not because as soon as I heard the slam I was out cold.

When I woke up my head was pounding. So much for sleeping this off. The room was bright as hell and I was still hot. I had no concept of time. I could hear someone downstairs, but I did not have the strength or desire to get up and see who it was. Hopefully I wasn't being robbed. If I was, they'd better keep their ass downstairs. I'm sick, not stupid, and will quickly grab my gun Halo and make some angels up in here.

Whomever it was started to come up the stairs. They were still talking so it wasn't a robber. I tried to make out the voice, but all I heard was grumbling. Hell, I could understand Charlie Brown's teacher better than this person. My door opened slowly. I could see the silhouette of three people. One was Jason. The other two were slimmer, shorter, and curvier.

"What's wrong, honey?"

It was Laila. He went and got backup. No fair!

I couldn't respond. I only moaned and groaned while struggling to sit up. My body collapsed back into the bed as it held me hostage. I became a prisoner in my own room and there was nothing I could do about it. This illness was not about to take me out, but it was doing a damn good job of keeping me down.

"Stop trying to get up!"

That must be Phoenix. I know she's not telling me not to get up. Not that I had the strength to move anyway. I gave up struggling to move and just stayed in my current position. They both straightened me up in bed.

"Alright, Jay, we got it from here." I heard Laila say. "You go do what you have to do. She'll be fine."

"Are you sure?"

"Dude, we got this!" I could see Phoenix pushing him out the room.

"Thanks, ladies. Call me if she needs anything. I'm serious."

"We will." Laila said.

After Jason left, the girls closed the blinds and laid beside me in the bed - Phoenix to my right and Laila to my left.

"What's the matter, sweetie?" Laila said.

"I bet you she's pregnant." Phoenix remarked sarcastically.

"Shut up!" I managed to get out.

I couldn't say anything else after that yet managed to let out a snicker while they laughed their asses off. I loved these two girls with all my heart. They are always there for me no matter what, even when I'm being hard-headed. I wanted to thank them for coming to my rescue, but my energy was spent. I leaned my head on Laila's shoulder and passed out.

When I woke up it was dark in the room. Phoenix and Laila were still in bed with me. They were sound asleep. Seeing them by my side made me realize just how lucky I am to have real friends that will do anything for me. Most people don't even have one person they can depend on. I am blessed to know that I have these two.

I felt a lot better than I did a few hours ago which, to me, seemed like a miracle. It was 4:51 in the morning and I knew they had to get home. Gently, I rocked them both until they woke up.

"Hey, sleepy heads!" I said. "Thanks for staying with me last night."

"You're welcome." Phoenix said. "It's what we do. What time is it?"

"Almost five in the morning."

"Really?" Laila asked. "So why did you wake us up?"

"Don't you two have to go to work?"

"Wren!" Phoenix got loud. "It's Saturday!"

"Shut up! No, it isn't."

Laila reached over the nightstand and grabbed my phone. It was too bright for me to see, but sure enough it was Saturday.

"Well ain't this about it!" I said. "How long have I been out of it?"

"Long enough to get your days mixed up!" Laila said. "Can we please go back to sleep now?"

Phoenix was already out.

"Wait, Laila, before you do, I want to ask you something."

She gave me the *make it quick* look.

"Do you think Phoenix was right? Could I be pregnant?"

"If so, I pray that you only have one child because what you just went through was scary as hell."

"Who are you telling?"

"Get some rest, Wren. We'll tackle that problem later."

"Wait, where's Jason?" I asked.

"He's in the other room. Want me to go get him?"

"No, that's okay. Thanks, Laila. You're the best."

"I know."

I snuggled up under my covers and was fast asleep.

The next day I made everyone a huge breakfast to thank them for taking care of me. GiGi, Nellie and Emma stopped by as well. They had been popping in and out through this whole ordeal. I thought I was just sick for a few hours. Turns out I was down for three days. I don't remember anything that happened while I was sick. The stories that were cycling over eggs, pancakes, sausage and grits had me in tears. Apparently, I'm a riot when I'm out of my mind.

"No, but the funniest part was her snap reaction when I told her she might be pregnant!" Phoenix roared in laughter.

"That's not funny!" I said.

"Would that be so bad, bae?" Jason asked.

The room went dead silent. We've never talked about our future together, so I never considered it. Was he serious, or was this one of his moments when he was fucking with me? It was hard to tell.

"I don't know. Would it?"

"Aww, that's so sweet!" Nelli said. "They're going to have a baby! I want to be a God-mother!"

"Stop it, Nelli!" GiGi said. "She's not pregnant. She just had one hell of a viral spell."

"Y'all are killing me with all of this baby talk." Emma said in a nasty tone. "Can we switch the subject, please?"

"What's up your ass?" Phoenix asked. "You've been acting bitchy since we got here."

"Who are you calling a bitch?"

"Stop!" GiGi said. "Emma, not here. Not now."

"What is that supposed to mean?" Emerald and Phoenix said, staring each other down.

Before anyone could respond Wren took control of the situation. She could sense there was tension between Emma and Phoenix and didn't want it to boil over. They've always had a love-hate relationship with each other. This must be one of their down times. As much as they fought each other she knew they'd kill for each other and that was more important. The best thing to do at this point was to diffuse the situation.

"Ladies, and yes, that's what we are, whatever the issue is can't be that serious. We go through this at least once a month. That's fine; it is what it is, but not today. I can't go from illness to recovery to court because y'all want to bash in each other's heads. Kill that noise, for real."

"She's right, Emma." Phoenix said. "Whatever your issue is with me can be handled later. Deal?"

Emma didn't want to cower, but she was outnumbered, and she knew it.

"Fine."

With that said we finished having a nice breakfast before everyone parted ways. That was one thing about our group that I appreciated. Whenever we had an issue with one another we always discussed it at the appropriate time. Now what these heifers do after they leave my house is on them. I'm sure they'll handle it properly…however that may be.

Once everyone left Jason and I had some one-on-one time. I felt bad for neglecting him while I was sick. Not that I had a choice, but I take pride in making sure my man is always happy. It was time for me to get back on my grind…literally.

We went upstairs to our room and I led him to the bed.

"Hey baby. I want to thank you for taking care of me." I said as I slid out of my silk robe.

"No problem, baby." He said. "That's why I'm here."

I slowly began to climb on top of him.

"I know, and I appreciate you for it. Now it's time for me to show you just how much I appreciate you."

Like a smooth operator I pierced his penis through my lips. He squirmed feverishly as I worked his magic stick in and out of my mouth. Sounds were coming from him that I'd never heard before. We had officially reached a new plateau. I switched gears from soft and slow to hard and fast. The change in speed made him twitch harder.

I took the tip of his penis and nibbled on it. His pre-cum tasted like caramel…my favorite flavor. It was one of the reasons why I called him Sugar Daddy. Damn he tasted so good.

"Baby, what are you doing to me?" He said between deep breaths.

"Shh…no talking." I commanded. "Just lay back and enjoy."

I damn near got lockjaw, but it was worth every ache and pain I felt later. In the thirty minutes I orally pleased him I made him cum twice.

"Oh shit!"

After the second bust he passed out. I got on top of him and continued to rock him to sleep. Even when limp he still had enough girth to make me squirt all over him. Light moans were coming from him as I sent myself into a massive climax.

"I love you, baby!" I squealed as I released all my love on his hot, sweaty body.

Exhausted and satisfied, I laid on top of him. I felt his arm slip around me and pull me close.

"I love you, too, baby."

That was all I needed to hear. We laid in bed holding each other for the next three hours. I slept like a baby wrapped up in his arms. Sometimes I fear losing him to someone else because he's so perfect…too perfect. He's a good provider always takes care of my every need and want, spoils me to no end, and he's painfully attractive. He has the type of body that makes women cry and men cringe. To top it all off he's completely mine.

At times I wonder what he sees in me. I used to ask him that question all the time until one night we got into a heated discussion about it. He could sense my insecurity and neither one of us were comfortable with it. I was given an ultimatum: either trust him completely or let him go. I loved him too much to leave him, so I vowed to never question his presence again. Instead, I made it my purpose to please him in every way possible. Not that I need to, but I want to because every day he unselfishly does the same for me.

When I woke up, I could feel the gentle touch of his tongue caressing my lower backside. He knew that was my sensitive spot. His finger lightly caressed my spine and slowly slipped into my vagina. His long, thick fingers sent my kitty purring uncontrollably. As his middle and forefingers massaged my internal cavern of love my clitoris was being pleasured by his thumb.

I proceeded to fondle my breast which turned me on even more. He stopped long enough to turn me on my back, gave me his beautiful smile with his gorgeous dimple and went back to working the kitty, this time while caressing my nipples with his tongue. What can I say? He loves how I taste.

Only thing I needed now was for him to penetrate my body, but I knew he wouldn't. He got enough pleasure out of finger fucking me, which I enjoyed, but I needed something stronger. I just might have to take advantage of him.

I found his sweet spot just behind his scrotum and started massaging it with my fingers. Lightly I went in circles which gave him an instant erection. The tip of his penis was dripping with my favorite caramel sauce. I caught it with my free hand and massaged it on my lips, slowly licking it off with my tongue. He leaned in for a kiss and that's when I struck. Masterfully I gyrated my hips with him on top of me, tenderly kissing him until I maneuvered him inside of me. Before he could notice I gripped his penis with my vagina and refused to let go.

"Damn, baby!" He puffed. "You got me."

I just bit his lip and went to work. I was half his size but at that moment I had twice his strength. I took him to depths he didn't know existed in me. The vibration created from his cum surging to the top only made me work harder. We were dripping wet from licking and sucking on each other. This, by far, was the best love making session we've had in a long time.

An hour in and I was coming for something like the tenth time. He was good at controlling his body, but I was ready to experience his massive explosion.

"I'm ready baby." I said with a quivering voice. "Explode in me!"

It only took ten long, deep strokes for him to fill me up with his love. We came at the same time; the mattress never stood a chance.

I got in the shower to clean up. My vagina was a little sore and stung as the water ran between my backside, but every moment was worth it. Once I was dressed Jason took me out to dinner. It was date night for us, although everything seemed to be happening backwards. We usually end with the love making session. I guess it's good to switch things up occasionally.

Phoenix

My friendship with Emerald was on the rocks, but I had no idea why. I hadn't done anything directly to hurt her and don't understand her current disdain towards me. Usually I know exactly what the problem is and address it accordingly. This time I'm at a loss. There is one person who might have a clue about Emerald's nasty attitude…Gainell.

"Hey girl, what's up?" Gainell said, answering the phone.

"Hey!" I responded. "What are you doing?"

"About to go shopping courtesy of Jordan. He pissed me off last night."

"Oh shit. How much is it going to cost him this time?"

"I'm feeling very forgiving, so only about ten stacks."

"You are a mess!" I laughed on the other end. "What's up with Emma? What did I do to her now?"

"What do you mean?"

"Don't play with me, Nelli. You know what I'm talking about. What was she going to confront me about yesterday at Wren's house?"

"Why are you still on that?" Gainell asked. "Let it go. You know how she is."

"I can't let it go because I don't know what to let go of, Nelli. You know something that I don't so spill it."

Gainell could sense the tension in my voice. I knew she wanted to tell me because she felt like I needed to know. On the other, she probably didn't want to get involved in yet another one of our dramas, and Emerald and I have had our fair share of issues with each other. The last one didn't end so well and she hated taking sides.

"Phoe, I love you, I really do, but if you want to know what stick is up Emma's ass this time you need to go straight to the source. Besides, truth be told I'm not completely sure. She tried to tell me, but I told her she needs to go to you."

"I can't stand you, heifer." I said in frustration.

"I love you, too. Call her and see what's up. I'm about to go burn up Neiman's."

"Red boots. Knee high. Size 7."

"Fuck you."

I just laughed. After hanging up with Gainell I thought about calling Emerald. It was bugging me that she had the audacity to be pissed off. She always comes up with a thousand different reasons to be angry, but none of them ever make any sense. Then again, Emerald's tantrums rarely ever made sense. After giving it some though, I decided against calling her. I need to see her face to face. I need to be able to look into her eyes and read her body language. Emerald is wiggly as a worm when she's hiding something. Gainell was right. It was time to go straight to the source.

Emerald lived a half hour away. During the drive, I thought about all the times our friendship was on the rocks. It was more common than I cared to admit and frankly I'm getting tired of the unnecessary and nonessential bullshit.

This wasn't something that was going on for a year or two. This had been the foundation of our 15-year friendship. Most of the time it was over something petty, which made it even worse. Sometimes, it was a big issue and sometimes it was my fault, but I'd never let Emerald know that. When it was my fault I always owned up to my mistakes and made no hesitation to apologize. Emerald soaked those moments up, knowing me apologizing was rare. It only got out of control a handful of times. I'm hoping this won't be one of them.

"God please don't let us go to blows, but if we do, let it be the last time."

I said a silent prayer as I edged closer to Emerald's house. I didn't even bother calling her. That would only give her time to prepare a guilt trip. If this were truly an issue, I wanted it to come out authentically; not some concocted scheme that Emerald came up with. I turned the corner on Emerald's street and saw her car in the driveway. She was home. The truth was only minutes away.

I pulled up behind Emerald's car. Most of the time she was in the back of her place so I wasn't worried about being seen. After saying another quick prayer I took a deep breath and got out of the car. Every step towards her door added a new butterfly in my stomach. I wasn't afraid of confronting Emerald. I was scared this may be the last nail in the proverbial coffin that would kill our friendship for good.

"It's now or never." I said under my breath.

I knocked on the door. Thirty seconds went by and there was no answer. The second time I knocked louder and longer. A few more seconds went by before the door swung open.

Emerald was standing on the other side of the screen door looking like she just rolled out of bed. Her hair was still wrapped up in a scarf, cotton robe tied tightly around her waist, dots of what appeared to be acne medicine were on her forehead and cheeks. I went from being nervous to amused and - without trying to be demeaning - let out a laugh.

"What's so funny?" Emerald said with an attitude.

"Girl, what the hell are you doing? It's the middle of the day. Why aren't you dressed?"

Emerald just stood at the door and gave no answer.

"Well can I at least come in?" I asked.

"Are you done laughing at me?"

I opened the screed door and walked past her. I'm not here for humor. This is about getting to the root of Emerald's issue with me. The last thing I need is another layer of bitterness on top of the one that already existed. We walked to the back room where we always hung out. Her living room was for show only.

"Listen we need to talk, Emma." I said as I sat on the couch.

"Talk about what?"

"What was wrong with you yesterday at Wren's house? You've had this attitude with me lately and I don't understand why. After talking with Nelli I was instructed to come to you. What do we need to talk about?"

"Damn her!"

"No, don't damn her. She didn't do or say anything wrong. You have an issue with me, so what is it this time?"

"My issue is with you being so negative all of the damn time!"

"What are you talking about? When have I been negative?" I sat back, waiting for the barrage of accusations to begin.

"The other week when you…"

"Wait a minute. You're ticked off at something that happened *weeks* ago? You can't be serious, Emma. You can't be." I tried to laugh it off, but I could see where this was going.

"Look, you asked me a question. Do you want me to answer it or not?"

I signaled for her to proceed.

"You have this bad habit, Phoe, of constantly complaining about this dude, that dude, or the other. Frankly, I'm tired of hearing about it. How can you be so ungrateful? Do you know how many women would kill to even gain attention from the type of men that you attract?"

"You mean like you?"

"What's that supposed to mean?"

"Let's be real, Emma. You're not mad that I was bitching about some man. You're mad because you don't have a man to bitch about."

Emerald shot up and immediately got in my face.

"Fuck you, Phoenix! Don't you dare sit there and try to judge me!"

When Emerald put her finger in my face it set me off. Instinctively, I grabbed her finger and twisted it. In retaliation Emerald slapped me with her free hand. That led to an all-out brawl in Emerald's back room. When I pushed Emerald she fell to the ground. I tried to jump on her, but she rolled out of the way. She grabbed a vase and broke it on my back.

"Oh, so we're going there?!" I puffed.

I ran toward Emerald ready to commit murder and slammed her against the wall. Repeatedly I punched her in the face until the rings on my fingers were covered in blood. Emerald tried to knee me in the stomach. She kept missing, so she grabbed my neck when I pulled back for another punch. Emerald squeezed her fingers into my neck so deep that it cut me.

"I'm done playing with you, bitch!" Emerald yelled and pushed me off her.

I fell to the ground and hit my head on the corner of the coffee table. Emerald turned to grab the bat she kept behind her couch. Before she could get it, I kicked the back of her knees and sent her sprawling to the floor. I started to kick her but stopped in mid swing.

"You know what, Emerald? I can't do this with you anymore." I said, fighting back tears. "This friendship is toxic. You're toxic. I'm too good of a person to deal with toxic people. I'm done with you."

Without saying another word, I stepped over Emerald and walked out of the house. Without looking back, I got in my car and pulled off. Tears immediately fell from my eyes. I may have won the fight, but I lost my best friend; this time for good. I felt like my heart had been ripped out my chest. I rushed home as fast as I could. I pulled in my driveway and allowed everything to hit me. The accusations. The fighting. The severing of our friendship. It was then I realized this truly was the end. That realization sent me into a panic attack.

Gainell

I returned home from shopping with my twin, Giuseppina. It's one of our favorite past times and we never get tired of it. We could spend all day going from luxury department store to jewelers to boutiques. GiGi and I were no stranger to the luxurious life. Our parents are partners in one of the nation's largest entertainment companies. They have their hands in everything from music to movies to television. We grew up in that industry but wanted something different for our lives. While we loved living it up as kids in the entertainment industry, GiGi and I had our sights set in a different direction: accounting.

I'm the Chief Financial Officer of a Fortune 500 company. I'm also the company's youngest and most intelligent CFO; having managed to save the firm millions of dollars in deals while making a couple of million in the process. The money is good and all, but for me it's not enough. I didn't just want to be a millionaire. My goal is to become a billionaire - yes, with a *B*. Between my position within the company, my real estate properties, and my investment portfolio I was well on my way to achieving that billion within a few short years.

My twin, Giuseppina, has a similar success story. Another master of numbers, she started her own accounting firm. Hundreds of businesses trust their books with her company and in the seven years she's been in business they've never made one mistake. To free up her time and energy she appointed someone else to be the CEO of the company. That way, she can enjoy overindulging on the things she loves: money, travel, and shoes. GiGi's shoe collection spans in the thousands. It's her worst overindulgence and the main reason why she worked so hard to build her business.

"Ciao doppia, l'ho fatta a casa." GiGi said on the other line.

"Buono!" I said.

GiGi must be happy because only three instances will bring out her Italian roots: excitement, anger, or really good sex. Turns out she received a call that one of her biggest deals yet just finalized. She just signed a multi-million-dollar client that was projected to be worth $78 Million dollars within the next twelve months.

When she shared the news I was so happy for her. I was also happy for me because whenever she scores a major deal I usually follow up with one of my own. Call it twin energy, synergism, whatever. I'm ready for my windfall. As she was telling me about her new deal Phoenix called my phone three times back to back. On the fourth call I knew something was up.

"I got to go, Bambino." She was my baby because I was born three minutes before her. "Phoenix is calling me."

"Okay, sis. Ti amo!"

"Ti amo! I love you!"

I hung up with GiGi and clicked to the other line.

"Hey girl! Did you talk to Emma?"

All I could hear was Phoenix crying and sobbing. I guess it didn't go well.

"I'm so done with that bitch it's not even funny." She finally said.

"What happened?"

Phoenix proceeds to tell me how their altercation went down. My heart ached for her. I knew she wanted an answer, but I'd never imagine their friendship would end this way. I could tell she was hurt, but I also knew her ego would not allow her to feel this pain for long. This would be her one and only vent about the situation. Afterwards, she would dismiss everything that just happened - even the parts that were her fault.

"I don't understand, Phoe. Why would you attack her?"

"She got in my face! What else was I supposed to do?"

"I understand that, but did you really have to get all in her ass like that?"

"Yes, I did!" She said defensively. "No one wrongly accuses me and gets away with it! Especially not some jealous filled bitch that doesn't have a pot to piss in or a window to throw it out!"

"Whoa! Calm down tiger! I'm not the culprit here."

"I know! I'm just so damn pissed at myself. I should have cut ties with that bitch a long time ago."

"Are you seriously done with her?"

There was a brief silence. For about thirty seconds I didn't hear anything on the other line. I knew she was gathering her thoughts. She was also pushing everything that just happened out of her system. Her prideful ways were kicking in; she refuses to let anything get the best of her. This was not going to be pretty.

"Phoenix. Are you there?"

A couple more seconds passed before she spoke.

"Yeah, I'm here."

"Are you going to answer my question?"

"I didn't hear you. What did you ask me?"

"Are you seriously done with her?"

"Her who?"

"Emma!"

"Yeah, that name doesn't ring a bell. Anyway, I have to go now. I'll call you later."

"Okay."

With that she hung up the phone. There was no use in talking any sense into her now. Once she makes a decision, she sticks with it. Besides, as much as I love Phoenix, I have my own life to focus on. And right now, my focus is on getting that multi-million dollar deal of my own. Call it healthy competition, but if GiGi can get a deal like that I should be able to get twice what she made.

I don't like to work on weekends, but I don't like to leave money on the table either. I called up Denise, the head of my financial executive team and told her it was a good time to follow up with one of our biggest clients that seemed to be on the fence. She wanted to wait until Monday, but I insisted she send out a communication now. This energy between my twin and I only last for so long and I didn't want to miss the opportunity. She said an email would go out immediately.

I went to the master bedroom and spread out the fifteen shopping bags I had accumulated from our shopping spree. One by one I pulled out the new items and put them away amid the hundreds of other items still tagged and unworn. The purpose of this shopping trip was not to feed my impulsive need for spending. It was a lesson I had to teach Jordan, who mistakenly called me a spendthrift. He wasn't lying, but one thing you don't do is try to call me out on my shit…especially if it's with my own money.

Jordan's intentions are genuine. I love him and want to marry him one day, but he just doesn't understand my lifestyle. Even though I make more than enough money to finance how I live, he feels that I sometimes go to exaggerated lengths to maintain my upkeep. Sure, at times I make drastic decisions, but I'm always careful to weigh the benefits against the risks. It makes him uncomfortable sometimes when I "rock the boat" so to speak, but I'll do what I have to do in order to get what I want. He's always telling me that the decisions I make are borderline illegal. He doesn't want his future wife to go to jail. I'm trying to see it from his point of view, but my desire for what I want clouds my judgment at times. My most recent attempt to score a deal was not only futile, but cost him somewhere in the region of about $23,000 and he doesn't even know it yet.

Between us, I make more money, but the difference is so small it's barely noticeable - except to him. Respectively, we tend to have very strong, competitive personalities that can – at times - get in the way of our relationship. I'll play around with him and bring up the fact that I make $20,000 more than he does. In his mind he's the true breadwinner because while I make more money, he works less hours and has more time. He only works 60 hours per week compared to my 80 plus hours. These arguments tend to become so intense that we won't speak to each other for days. Someone always buckles and apologizes – and it's usually him. Then we commence to having the best make-up sex on the planet.

After putting away my newly purchased items I took Jordan's black AmEx card and placed it in his drawer in the exact position I found it. My mind turned back to Phoenix and Emerald. I couldn't believe their friendship spanning over 15 years was finally over. *This is some bullshit!* There was no way something as petty as Phoenix complaining about a man spurred such bitterness and hostility. Something else was going on with Emerald and I was determined to find out what it was.

I changed out of my designer jeans, cashmere sweater, and Louboutin boots and switched to a Nike jump suit and tennis shoes. The last thing I needed to do was bruise Emerald's already fragile ego by showing up looking all flashy. It was bad enough I would be pulling up in a seven series BMW, but Emerald was used to seeing my car. No need in adding insult to injury.

On the way to Emerald's house I received a call from Laila.

"Nelli!" Laila screamed in excitement on the other line. "I've met my husband!"

"Girl, please! You've only met your flavor of the week!"

"No, seriously!"

Laila proceeded to talk my ear off about her newest prospect. I listened patiently as it was a good distraction from what was currently going on. After ten minutes of Laila's non-stop ranting I was finally able to get a word in the conversation.

"You really like this guy, huh?"

"Yeah, and I think he likes me, too!"

"Wait. You *think* he likes you?"

"Don't start, Nelli." Laila said sternly.

"Hey, you called me all excited. I would never take that away from you." *Even if it means you're being a complete moron.* I thought.

"You're being condescending again."

"No, seriously. I know how you feel about finding the right guy. If you think this can go somewhere, I don't want to be the one to plant the seed of doubt in your head. Really, Laila, if you're happy then I'm happy for you. Shoot, if he makes you happy then go for it. Just make sure you're receiving what you're giving, that's all."

"And she slips into big sister mode."

"And you love me for it."

"Anyway, what are you doing?" Laila asked.

"Diva down."

"Who is it this time? Emerald? Phoenix? I know it's not you."

I proceeded to fill Laila in on the fight that ensued just a few hours ago. She was shocked, but not surprised, that it went as far as it did. Phoenix has complained to her about Emerald on several occasions. She's wanted to end the friendship for quite some time, but never had a valid reason to let it go. As far as Laila was concerned, Phoenix saw her exit and took it without a second thought.

"Nelli, if I were you I'd just leave it alone. You already know how those two can be and the last thing you want is for them to force you to pick sides."

"Now you know I don't choose sides, Laila. That's the last thing on my mind. I just want to see where Emerald's head is and how she feels about the situation. I can't have one side looming in my head without knowing the other person's version. I'm just going to talk to her, that's all."

"Okay, but tread lightly, grasshopper! You're entering a minefield with a lot of hidden strong emotions. Don't blow yourself up. I need you in my wedding!"

"Girl, you are crazy!" I laughed. "Learn who the guy is before you take on his last name."

"You're such a mood killer!" Laila joked.

"Whatever! I'm pulling up to Emma's house. I'll call you later. Maybe I can talk some sense into you then."

"Good luck with Emma. Remember, tread lightly."

I hung up with Laila and walked up to Emerald's house. I knocked on the door and waited for Emerald to answer. After waiting for about a minute I knocked again. Emerald never came to the door. I turned to see if the door was unlocked and it opened.

"Emma?" I yelled in the house. "It's Nelli. Are you in there?"

Light sobs came from the back room. I closed the door and made my way to the back room. Emerald was still on the floor where Phoenix left her.

"Emma? Are you okay, sweetie?"

I kneeled next to her on the floor. Staring straight ahead, Emerald didn't respond. She was too disconnected from reality. The bruises on her face and the dry blood surrounding her nose and lower lip told me just how intense her fight was with Phoenix.

"Come on, sweetie. Let's get you on the couch."

I tried to get Emerald to stand, but she wouldn't budge. Using all my strength, I finally got Emerald on the couch. She laid down, too lifeless to sit up. My heart ached at the sight of her. She looked so beat down and broken. Not from the fight, but from the loss of her best friend.

I went to get some towels to clean her up. Dabbing at her face, I gently cleaned off the blood and wiped away the tears that were now incessantly streaming down her face. The more tears I wiped the more she began to cry. Emerald grabbed my arm. She turned to me with sad, puppy dog eyes.

"She's gone, Nelli. My best friend is gone and I'll never get her back."

Emerald began crying uncontrollably. I'm not one for emotions but watching just how badly Emerald was breaking down tugged at my heart. I sat and held her tightly as the guilt, sadness, and loss flooded out. There was nothing I could've said to calm her down. I quietly sat while she let everything out.

For the next two hours that's what Emerald did. In intervals she went from crying uncontrollably to being eerily silent. I would attempt to straighten up the back room whenever she was calm. There was broken glass and busted vases all over the floor, and cracks in the wall. Emerald already didn't have a lot to begin with. Once she realizes that she destroyed some of her most precious items she'll spiral out of control again. I made a note of the items that were broken so I could replace them for her.

As day turned into night Emerald began to calm down. Little by little she started asking why their friendship had to end. The questions weren't directed towards me specifically. She was mainly questioning herself. I didn't interject; I let Emerald work through the situation out loud and in her own head. My only role at this point was to be there in case she broke down again, and to be there when she's ready to talk.

"How did we get to this point?"

"Do you really want the answer to that, Emma?"

Emerald sat for a minute before she replied. Deep inside, she already knew what brought them to this point, but since no one else verbalized it she could always justify her need to be right. If I confirmed what she already knew she would no longer be able to play the victim role.

"I already have the answer."

"What are you going to do about it?"

"What can I do, Nelli? You know how Phoenix is; once she says she's done that's it."

We sat in silence for a while longer. Emerald was beside herself with grief. I wanted to be with her, but I was also ready to go home. It was almost midnight and nothing had changed. We never came to a resolution and I still didn't know Emerald's side of the story. What I did know was that, once again, Emerald's character showed up and showed out and this time it cost her Phoenix's friendship.

"Listen, Emma, I'm about to go. Don't take this to heart just yet. Give Phoe a few days to cool off and then give her a call. Let her know how you feel and that you're sorry."

"But I'm not sorry, Nelli! I'm tired of her constant complaining and feeling like everything should be her way or no way at all."

I sat back in disbelief. How could she be so distraught if she wasn't sorry?

"Then why in the hell are you spazzing? If you're sick of it, then why does it matter if she's your friend or not?"

"It matters because she deserves better, but at the same time she needs to know everything isn't about her."

"You're not making any sense right now."

"Well it makes sense in my head!" Emerald snapped back.

"Get some rest, girl. You've had one hell of a day."

I stood up to leave. Emerald went into her own world again. I didn't want to bother her so I just left, locking the door behind me. *Them bitches are crazy.* I started my car and pulled off, leaving Emerald to fend for her friendship - and her sanity - alone.

Wren

"It looks like everything is fine, Wren." My doctor said. "You must have just had a bad case of food poisoning or something."

In a way that made me feel better, but it was still disheartening he couldn't find the cause of my illness. I left my doctor's office with a clean bill of health, praying that whatever caused me to get that sick will never enter my body again.

"At least I'm not pregnant." I said half-heartedly as I pulled out of the parking lot.

I went straight home because I only had one more day to get some rest before I had to return to work. Even though I had a lot of errands I needed to run they could wait. Hell, they waited this long. What's another day or two? My bed was calling me, and I was bound and determined to answer it.

When I got to the house Jason wasn't there. It wasn't a big deal because I knew he would come in sooner or later. The first thing I did was check the voice mail. The first two messages were from Gainell. She said something about a fight between Emerald and Phoenix. I'll have to call her about that later. The next message was dead silence which was weird. The last message caught me off guard. I wasn't sure if I heard it right, so I replayed it.

"What the fu…"

I know that voice anywhere. It was Jason. I kept repeating the message over and over, wondering what he was trying to say. I checked to see what number he called from, but it was unlisted. This wasn't sitting right with me. I replayed the message again. This time I swore I could hear a female snickering in the background. There weren't enough replays in the world at that moment. The more I imagined that voice the stronger I heard it. At this point I was livid and called his cell phone.

>He didn't answer.
>I tried to call again.
>Still no answer.
>*Alright, Wren, keep it together. Don't start flipping out.*

My ego went into full attack mode. In a matter of seconds, he went from being a loving, caring boyfriend to every derogatory name outside of the one his momma gave him. Who was that bitch in the background and what fucking right did she have to call my phone? How did she get my number? What was he hiding from me that he couldn't answer his phone?

I started blowing his phone up. After the third time my calls started going straight to voicemail. *Oh, so he's going to play that game now?* Fine, it was on. Angela Bassett and Left Eye better look out because the tirade I was about to commence would make their fires look like sparklers. It only took me ten minutes to gather every article of clothing, shoes, jewelry, credit cards; you name it and toss that shit into garbage bags. My house was a mess, but I didn't care. I tossed his shit in the trunk of his precious old school Chevy Impala and went for a drive.

The entire time I kept trying to call him. I never left a message because I knew he would sense my anger and try to stop me from spazzing out. Not that it mattered; I was already on ten and his lack of response only made it worse. That snicker replayed in my head repeatedly. Tears started streaming from my eyes. This bastard was cheating on me. If he wasn't then why wouldn't he answer my calls? How long has this been going on? Who was she and what made her better than me?

I couldn't take the questions anymore. He was going to pay for making a fool out of me. It was three in the morning and the roads were deserted. I pulled into Hamilton Arms

Apartments. They're known for their landscaping, but that was the least of my concerns right now. I was here for one thing and one thing only - the lake in the middle. They were restructuring part of the parking lot. Certain sections were coned off from cars because the angle created a hazard of cars slipping into the lake.

That's exactly what I wanted.

I had to act quickly because security patrols the area every hour. I rolled down all the windows and placed the car in neutral. Right next to me was a big rock. I threw it in the driver's side and it landed on the pedal just enough to get the car rolling. Forget the fire; I'd love to see his face when they catch this big fish. Slowly his car rolled down the hill and into the lake. It was so smooth it barely made a sound. A smile came across my face.

Payback is a bitch!

I went through the complex and came out on the other side. Within ten minutes I hailed a cab and was on my way home. My story was already put together. I just hope he wasn't at the house or my cover would be blown. When I pulled up, he still wasn't there. Perfect. I got in my car and went for a drive, you know, to warm up my engine. Forty-five minutes later I pulled up to the house, went inside, and immediately called the police.

"I've been robbed and my boyfriend's car is missing!"

"We'll send an officer out right away." The dispatcher said.

Now I could leave a message.

"Baby, you need to come home right away. We've been robbed and your car is gone!"

Let's see how quickly he responds to that.

Phoenix

Emerald has been calling me non-stop since our fight. As far as I was concerned there was nothing to talk about. She attacked me and I wasn't going to let her do that any longer. Fifteen years of this bullshit was enough. It was time for me to find a new best friend, or at least some different people to hang around. It had to be someone outside of our group for now until all this drama calms down.

Making new friends is easy for me. Keeping them - well – that's something different. Most of the time they just fade away, but sometimes I encounter a crazy girl or guy that I must put in their place.

That wasn't a primary focus for me now. I needed to get myself together and rid my surroundings of anything that even remotely reminds me of that girl. I am too good of a person to allow such fuckery in my life. If it weren't for me, she wouldn't have half of the stuff in her life that she does. She should be grateful that I stuck around for as long as I did. But that chapter is closed now. The book has been returned and I have no desire to check it out again.

This was nothing that a shopping spree couldn't fix. After all, I can actually afford to splurge whenever I wanted, unlike that broke hoodrat. I should feel sorry for her; she was nothing before I came into her life. Now that I'm gone, she'll be nothing again. Oh well, that's her problem, not mine.

Now that our friendship is over I feel like a weight has been lifted from my shoulders. No more carrying her around, enabling her weaknesses. Although she does a pretty good job of that on her own. Damn it, why am I still thinking about her?

Stop it, Phoenix! It's over!

Right, it's over, so don't sweat it anymore. It's time to shift my thoughts to something more meaningful. Or at least create a distraction. I need something to dull my senses…or someone. I picked up the phone to call Summer.

"Hello?" Summer answered in a somber tone.

"Hey, girl! How have you been?"

"I'm cool. What's up?"

"I haven't heard from you in a while so I wanted to check in and see how things were going with you."

"Oh, you know. Same shit, different day."

I had to laugh. Summer reminds me so much of Eeyore. She's always so dull and depressing. Not because she feels bad. She just has no energy or desire. Summer is a special kind of lazy; it's not that she doesn't try to be proactive. Her issue stems from childhood so she's conditioned with a one-and-done mindset. Even if her first attempt at something isn't successful she refuses to keep trying until she gets it right.

"I bet. What are you doing today? I'm going shopping and want you to go with me."

"No thanks. I don't feel like doing anything today."

"Why not?"

"I'm just not in the mood. I got some bad news and I need to take it in."

"Oh no. What happened?"

"I got turned down for a speaking engagement."

"What? That's crazy! They turned you down?"

"Well, they said I could be a backup in case one of the headline speakers couldn't make it."

"What's wrong with that?"

"I don't do backup, Phoe, you know that. I just said forget it."

"Summer, I love you and you know this, but you are out of your mind. You keep dropping everything after one lousy rejection! What is wrong with you?"

"Nothing is wrong with me. What's wrong with them?"

Summer's voice remained monotonic throughout the entire conversation. I knew I wasn't going to get anywhere with her.

"Girl, don't let them kill your talent like that. Keep trying. Your break will come sooner or later. I'll stop by to check on you later, okay?"

"Sure."

That was one sad conversation I just had and it did nothing to boost my morale. Everyone else was either not answering their phone or at work. I guess I would have to conquer this feeling on my own. Before my inner chatter could start again I got in my car, blared my music as loud as it could go, and headed towards the mall.

My outfit was on point. I was wearing my dark denim skinny jeans covered by my thigh high black books, a matching black blazer with a thin, white blouse underneath. My micro-braids were wavy and flowing, complementing the shape of my face. My figure put Coke bottles to shame. Even underneath my blazer you could see my 38C bust line. The stares and whistles I got from men felt good. The compliments from women felt better. The snide stares and hidden comments from females felt the best.

After spending an hour at the mall my ego was rebuilt. Having others acknowledge my greatness always works. When genuine strangers compliment and flirt with you it's a sure sign that you still got it. Not that I didn't already know that. However, confirmation is always good. By the time I left the mall I was on cloud nine. Everything that happened with Emerald and that conversation with Summer were both far from my mind. I was back to being my fabulous self; no need to backtrack.

Summer

Maybe Phoenix is right. I thought after I hung up the phone with her. Maybe I should accept the offer to be a backup speaker. After all, it's better than no speaking position at all. Not that I'm hurting for the money, but I really have this knack for motivating people. It's always the least likely person to do something for others. But that option did something to me. It made me feel like I wasn't good enough. It put me in second place to someone else on the panel.

I never did like second place. My disdain for coming up behind another person stemmed as far back as my childhood. My parents were always pushing me to be first, to be the best. They took the fun out of everything that I did. It got so bad that I started to purposely lose games, track meets, and contests just to piss them off. That was my initial reason, but somewhere along the line losing became a habit; one that I don't like and have been trying to break ever since.

Oh well, what's the use? Maybe this isn't my true calling at all. All the books say if it's really a passion and your calling it will come effortlessly. So far, the only thing that comes effortlessly to me is difficulty and disappointments. I've had enough of those to last me five lifetimes. It would be nice to get something different for a change. I know that starts with me, but damn, what else do I need to change? At this rate I won't be Summer anymore. If that's what it takes to live a halfway decent life then I might as well check out right now.

My only saving grace from suicide is the fact that I'm not too big on spending eternity in hell because of a childhood glitch. Not that I'm completely sure there's another hell in existence. The life I'm currently living is pretty damn close to its description, but instead of fire and brimstone I have fearfulness and breakdowns. Yes, pretty damn close indeed.

There isn't much to my life really. I do just the bare minimum to get by. While my girls are wildly fly, fabulous, and successful here I am sitting like a bump on a log. It's okay though, they still love me and I love them all dearly. That's the beautiful thing about our group. No matter who has what we're all there for each other. Sure, we fight, but what group of girls do you know that doesn't fight every now and then?

Oh no, I'm doing it again; slipping into the deep, dark abyss of depression. I need to head this off before it gets bad and they find me laying in a pile of my own shit again. Long story. My recent prescription of Xanax should do the trick. I'm only supposed to take one, but I know my body better than the doctor. Two pills and a shot of tequila usually do the trick. In almost a ritual fashion I pop the two pills, chase them with good ole' Jose, and wait for the magic to begin.

The process is kind of sickening. It takes about half an hour for everything to hit me. Once I throw up, I'm good. My philosophy is that regurgitating is my body's way of ridding itself of the negative energy. The liquor makes it easier to release the negativity. And since most of the medicine is immediately ejected it's better to take two pills than one.

Now I'd never tell my doctor or anyone else that I was doing this. They would probably have me committed. At any rate, it works for me and has for months. No sense in stopping now. I'm feeling a little perkier so maybe I'll take Phoenix up on that shopping trip after all.

Voice mail. I think in irritation. Of course she'd decide not to answer when I call her. Now if it were the other way around there would be hell to pay. I guess she went without me. That's cool, I'll call Wren and see what she's been up to since she's been isolated lately. Usually that's not a good sign. Time to check up on my girl.

Hey, you've reached Wren...

Where in the hell is everyone at that they can't answer their phones? I wasn't sure but the last thing I wanted to do was sit around and waste a good feeling. Looking around my house it hit me that I hadn't done any deep cleaning in a while.

It wasn't exciting, but add some music and more Jose' and I can turn anything into a party. But first I needed some supplies. On my way out the door I heard a knock. I answered and Jerome was standing at my door with a fresh bag of kush, a sealed bottle of Ciroc, and a stiff dick waiting just for me.

    Let the party begin.

Wren

"Tell me what happened again?" Jason asked me for what seemed like the hundredth time.

"I'm tired of reciting the story, Jay. It's not going to change. Here!" I said as I tossed the police report at him. "Read it for your damn self!"

I turned to walk away, but he grabbed my arm.

"I'm sorry, baby. I know you're frustrated. I just don't understand how all of my shit is gone, but most of yours is still here."

A very deep, sinister laugh slipped through my pursed lips. He was going to regret that comment for a long time.

"What are you trying to say? That your shit missing is my fault? Or that my shit is so worthless no one wants it? Or maybe it's a combination of the two! You have clearly lost your ever-loving mind!"

"Here we go!"

"No, bastard, here I go! How dare you sit there and make it seem like it was my fault your shit got stolen? You keep asking me where I was that night…where the fuck were you?"

I never did get a straight answer as to his whereabouts that night.

"What the fuck do you mean? You know good and damn well where I was!"

"Then why didn't you answer your phone when I initially called you? Why did it suddenly shoot to voicemail? You knew I was calling you; why didn't you call back?"

"Here we fucking go again! For the last fucking time, Wren, I wasn't with no bitch!"

My voice calmed down instantly.

"When did I say you were?"

The room got so silent I could hear his heart racing and his breathing turn into panting. He was trying his hardest to keep a straight face, but the guilt covered him like the Masked Marauder. If I started talking now it would interject with karma working for me, so I stood there…silently…patiently…and waited for a response.

"Look, baby, I'm sorry. That's usually what these silly arguments mean. It's just that you're always accusing me of doing something or someone behind your back and I'm tired of that."

"But here's the thing, Jason. I haven't accused you of anything in over a year. I haven't even hinted that I was suspicious. So, tell me, what makes you think that's what this is about? I thought the focus was on your stuff and your car? Where did another person some from?"

Once again, he sat speechless. He was digging his own grave and didn't even know it. I never mentioned the voice mails I received or the mysterious voice in the background of one of those messages. I never mentioned any of that since I discovered it. It's been a week and I've kept my lips shut tight. I guess the image of his car slowly slipping into that lake - a lake they still haven't investigated - was good enough for me. Watching him sweat his draws out trying not to confess is just icing on an already sweet enough cake.

"I can't do this with you right now."

In frustration, or perhaps overwhelming guilt, he got up and left the room. I didn't try to stop him, for if I did then I would play right into his trap. He's not slick; he's trying to lay a guilt trip so he can oh-so-casually turn this around on me. That's not going to happen. Not this time. Time for me to wind down and see what ratchetness will grace my screen today. Real life for me is exciting, but now I'm ready to step into someone else's drama for once. I need a break from my own.

Giuseppina

  This new client of ours is insane! The ink hasn't dried on the contract yet and they're already making outrageous requests. I'm all for bending over backwards to make someone happy, but I need a bigger kickback for their high demands.
  I guess that's the price for having such a successful business. I must admit it was all inspired by Nelli. When I see her command a client without their knowledge and get everything she wants - and a few surprise trinkets thrown in for good measure - I knew I wanted that lifestyle, too. Although with her it was solely about the money. Me, I want that and more! I've received bonuses, free international trips and cruises, high fashion clothes and shoes, and the purses…it all leaves you speechless!
  My clients do treat me well, even this new nutcase, so in the end it's always worth it. You can never have too much of the luxurious lifestyle. And it comes so effortlessly; it's almost a crime how easy this is. When they say what you focus on expands, they were not lying. I've always envisioned myself living this lifestyle. Ever since Nelli and I were little girls we knew wealth and abundance was our birthright. Our parents had it, but they lost it all due to an embezzlement scam that occurred when we were fifteen. It took seven years for that case to clear up and my father's former partners to be convicted. By then my poor dad had ran himself into the ground from stress, drinking, and smoking too much. He never got a chance to rebound. He passed away from cirrhosis of the liver three weeks after the verdict was delivered. At least he got to see those bastards get what they deserved.
  Nelli and I have been taking turns being there for our *Madre*. Just last year she decided that in her old age she wanted to live out the rest of her years with her family in Venice, Italy. Our mother is a purebred feisty Italian. She moved here to pursue the *American Dream* and, in the process, met our father

who is biracial with African American and European lineage. Together they built a successful business in the entertainment industry. That was back when Hollywood ruled everything. We had the best of everything and never wanted for nothing. That all went south on March 14, 1992. My father's accountant called him in for an emergency. When he arrived, the IRS had seized everything: equipment, accounts, files - you name it, they took it from us. It turned out that my father's partners, who were also the Chief Financial Officer and the Chief Organizational Officer, were skimming from the top and taking funds from high profile clients without accounting for it.

  For the first three years my father painstakingly attempted to clear his name. It was during this investigation that the IRS, and my father, discovered what was happening behind closed doors, in secret meetings, without CEO approval. The next four years he sat through court hearings, lawyer meetings, testimonies, everything to put those two scumbags in jail. He was upset that they stole from his company, but he was livid that they stole from his family. When the IRS seized everything all financial accounts, including both of my parent's personal accounts, were frozen.

  It was a devastating time for us all. What hurt the most is that it killed my father. He was my best friend and I miss him so much. I'm sure Nelli and my mother do, too, but we had a special relationship. I was his shadow and followed him everywhere. Maybe it was the tomboy in me when I was a kid, but we did all the father-and-son type things together. We would go hiking, fishing, play sports, go to games, and work on all sorts of projects. The day he died broke my heart. From that moment I vowed to never trust anyone with my money. Even in my own company I watch over everything like a hawk. Lack will never overtake me or my family again.

  My mother, God bless her heart, tried her best to move on after his passing. She would do well until the milestones came: his birthday, their anniversary, the day they started their first company, her birthday, the day of the court ruling, and finally the day of his passing. She went through this vicious cycle for a decade. We didn't know it, but it was slowly eating away at her. As time went on, she got good at hiding her feelings. On the tenth anniversary of my father's passing she took us out to dinner.

"Girls, it's been ten years since my Poopsi passed." That was her name for my father. "I miss him dearly."

"We know, Madre." Nelli said. "We miss him, too."

"I dream of him, you know. At least once a week he comes to see about me."

"That's sweet." I said.

"It's not sweet. It's reality. He's always looked out for us as a family and he continues to do so from beyond. Wherever he led me I willingly followed."

We sat there and smiled as she looked beyond the stars in the sky. It was a clear night for an outside meal next to the ocean. The weather was perfect, with a light breeze that gently blew at the tear that tried to escape her eye. She finally broke her silence.

"Girls, my time here in America has been wonderful, but it's time for me to go home."

My heart dropped. Immediately I started to protest.

"Mom, don't talk like that! It's not time for you to die yet! Where are you getting this nonsense?"

She laughed, but I was serious. My own feisty Italian started to come out. Good thing hers was under control.

"I'm not dying, Giuseppina. Not yet anyway."

"Then what are you talking about?" Nelli asked.

"I'm ready to go back to Venice. I'm ready to get back to *mi famiglia*!"

"But momma," Nelli began to protest, "We're your family!"

"Yes, you are *mi belle figlie*. But my time is almost up and when I go, I want to be in my homeland. That's where my Poopsi will meet me."

"Mom, wait!" I protested. "Can we talk about this?"

"We can, but my decision is made. I've already made arrangements. I'd like to leave by the end of the year."

Her decision was made, and we knew there was no changing her mind. While I didn't understand her reasoning I had to respect my mother's wishes.

"Qualunque sia il vostro cuore desidera, la madre. Whatever your heart desires."

My mother gave me the warmest smile. She was truly at peace with her decision. That's all I needed to be at peace as well.

Emerald

  I took Nelli's advice and waited a week before I attempted to contact Phoenix. I've known her for years and her pride will not let her sulk over anyone or anything for longer than a week. If she hasn't forgiven me by now, then I can chalk it up as a severed friendship. Without delay I picked up the phone.
  She better answer.
  The phone rang and rang. When it finally picked up my heart skipped a beat. I didn't know if it was her or the voice mail. Silence pierced through the other end of the phone. And then…dial tone.
  Shit!
  I guess this was the end. It's funny how she's able to throw away fifteen years of friendship over some useless dick. That's what it all boils down to; he was the reason we started beefing in the first place. Well I hope he was worth it, but they usually aren't worth the Cottonelle I use to wipe the shit off my ass. It's all good though. I got her number. If she thinks she can come up in my house, break my shit, and walk out with no consequences or repercussions she has another thing coming. I'm about to make her life a living hell.
  For the rest of the afternoon I concocted up schemes to get back at Phoenix. None of them had an order or a deadline to complete. I would strike when the time was right and opportunity presents itself. It's time I finally broke her prideful and egotistical ass down for good.
  There is one thing I can do immediately to get this revenge train moving along. Phoenix is very private and doesn't give out her phone number to anyone. This guy at our gym, Myron, has been trying for months to talk to her. She will not give him the time of day. Literally, he tried to ask her for the time and she completely blew him off. Myron is not the finest thing walking, but he's not Yoda either. Her resistance

could have something to do with the fact that he's married, but that's never stopped her before. I think now would be the perfect time to hook them up. The next time I see his car at the gym I'll be sure to do just that. In fact, he should be there now. I could use a good workout.

When I pulled up to the gym he was there. The parking lot was so packed that no one would notice me slipping the note under his windshield.

Patience is a virtue. Give me a call. 404-555-1629. Phoenix.

I placed the note in an envelope - even sealed it with a kiss – and slipped it under the wiper blade. I walked into the gym, not saying a word. The battle has begun.

Every machine in the building felt my presence as I worked out harder and longer than ever before. There was a lot of built up stress inside of me. It was time for a release and the gym gave me just that. My favorite trainer, Chauncey, was working the late shift. One by one the workout addicts began to leave. Eventually it was just Myron, Chauncey, Laurie the assistant manager, and I. We all knew each other well. This was perfect. I was in great company and I would be able to catch Myron's response when he got the note.

It was five minutes to closing time. Laurie left Chauncey in charge to lock up. Myron went to the locker room to change. I went to the women's locker room to do the same. Chauncey said he would give us a few extra minutes since he still had to wipe down all the machinery. When I passed the men's shower room I could hear Myron humming. He had a sexy voice; one that started to make me feel some type of way. It was hypnotic and led me to take a detour, dressed only in a towel, and follow its sound.

Peering around the corner I could see his silhouette in the shower stall. Myron was built like a stallion. The outline of his body was cut perfectly. Suddenly, I wanted him. Then he turned to the side and I could see he had a full blown erection;

at least seven inches. I know that doesn't seem like a lot, but I could work with it. The next thing I knew every inch of my thick, 5'7" frame was pressed up against his backside. When he turned around, I was sure he wouldn't be pleased with my approach. Damn was I wrong.

Sizing him up, I was totally off by two inches. He was much bigger, and thicker, than I thought. Secondly, he was more than happy to see me. With one swift move he pulled my hair, pinned me to the shower wall, and tongued me down like he was thirsty for affection. I met his aggressiveness with an equally passionate kiss of my own. I stood against that wall as his lips explored every nook and crevice of my body.

Then he picked me up and, as I wrapped my legs around his neck, proceeded to tongue down my second set of lips. This internal sweeping sensation sent me into another world. Thank God for the grips on the shower doors or we both would have surely face planted. When he stopped, I unwrapped my legs and slid down his body straight onto his pole. It was a beautifully executed move with no mishaps. The next five minutes were undoubtedly the best quickie session in my life.

Just before he came Myron pulled out and in swift motion I completed the action with my mouth, sucking out every protein-filled child that I could. As he regained his composure, I sent those same children down the drain - I am not the swallowing type - and rinsed my mouth out with the steaming hot water that was still caressing our bodies. He looked down at me with guilty eyes. Before he could say a word I put my finger to his lips.

"Shh. This will be our little secret."

With those final words, I lightly kissed him on the cheek and went to the women's shower room to clean myself up. My revenge was off to a good start. When the water hit my body the urge for pleasure returned. I was still tingling from Myron's penis and wanted more. As the stall filled up with steam I started pleasing myself, shifting my thoughts from

Myron to Chauncey. What would it feel like to have Chauncey inside of me? That innocent thought caused me to release three more times before I became frustrated. Finger fucking wasn't my thing unless it was someone else's fingers doing the fucking.

I'll see you later, man!

I heard Chauncey say goodbye to Myron in the background. I quickly stepped out of the shower. This was my opportunity to attack. Granted everything started with Myron; it was now up to Chauncey to finish it. I could hear him call my name from the door.

"Are you okay in there, Emerald?"

"Not really. Can you come here, please?" I said in a desperate tone.

"Are you decent?"

He was so cute and innocent with his countrified self. I never did answer his question, nor did he wait for a response. When he came around the corner I was sitting in a chair, the towel slowly slipping down my body, barely covering my breasts. The look on my face told him exactly what I wanted. Lucky for me, he was more than willing to give it.

There was no need for foreplay; I already took care of that with Myron. I motioned for him to come closer. He willingly obliged. While standing in front of me I unbuckled his belt and pulled down his pants. He sat down on the bench behind him and I straddled my body over his erect penis. He wasn't as long as Myron, but he was thicker which - for me - was better. Feeling the presence of his stiff penis enter my already slippery wet vagina caused me to let out an involuntary moan.

Chauncey loved this moment as much as I did. He was kissing my neck and squeezing my breast as he repeatedly thrust himself inside of me. I leaned back a little to give him a different feel. That sent him into another tirade of fucking me erratically. It started to hurt, but in a good way. When I couldn't take it anymore I pulled my body closer to his and began to slowly grind on him. He slowed down to match my rhythm. This pace was more like love making, which started to feel weird and good at the same time. I mean, I liked Chauncey and all, but that wasn't the point of having him inside of me. Or was it?

    I looked up for a brief second and though I saw someone walk pass the door. It was hard to see because of the lockers, but I didn't give it a second thought. Chauncey pulled my hair back and gave me a passionate kiss. He slowed down even more so he could go even deeper. Each push made me close my eyes tighter. He paused long enough for me to look and see Myron leaning against the locker. Half grinning, I noticed him putting on his wedding ring. He must have left it in the shower stall. I smiled at him and with the next intense thrust closed my eyes. When I opened my eyes he was gone.

    Chauncey came inside of me before he could pull out. I guess we got caught up in the moment. I slowly lifted off his penis, clinching my vaginal walls during the process. That caused a couple of extra squirts to come out of him. He leaned back on the bench and covered his face with his hands. I reached for the washcloth I used while in the shower and cleaned him up, completing the job with a few strokes of head. The remnants of cum that came out tasted like chocolate. Oh yeah, I could have fun with him.

    "Girl, you crazy!" He said as he pulled up his pants.

    "Maybe."

    He walked out of the locker room and I finished getting dressed. I worked out in more ways than one tonight and was ready to go home and crash. I gathered my stuff, put it in my gym bag, and walked towards the front door. Any normal chick would probably feel some type of way if she acted like I just did. For me, I was cool and content with my actions. I had hidden stress that needed to be released and picked the perfect men to help me do just that. For a moment I felt like Laila. She would be so proud of me right now. I laughed at the thought as I began to walk out. Chauncey met me at the door.

"Thanks for helping me out back there." I said. "Maybe we can do it again sometime."

"That's what's up."

He leaned down to give me a kiss. The intensity behind it assured me that there was more to what we just did than straight fucking. I might be okay with that…one day. Right now, it wasn't in the cards, but it's nice to know I have that option. He is my number one contender and now that I know how good he is with the dick he was also some serious competition.

"Don't get me started again." I warned. "I can always go for another round."

"Here's my direct number." He handed me a card. "Call me when you're ready."

"I sure will."

I made one last grab for his penis before heading out the door. He was rock hard again. Damn that man is amazing. Walking to my car I noticed the envelope I put on Myron's car on the ground. It was ripped in half. Did I really fuck him so good that he no longer wanted Phoenix? If so, that would surely bruise her ego - and score me some extra points. I smiled and got in my car.

Staring at Chauncey's number I made a mental note to give him a call in a few days. I locked his number in my phone for future use. I pulled off and crossed the parking lot to go to the pharmacy. After purchasing my Plan B, I headed home, knowing that not only was I not going to be pregnant, but I was ahead of my plan to ruin Phoenix forever.

Laila

Darren and I have been spending a lot of time with each other for the past week. The more time we spend together the more I start to believe we might have a chance. Everything seemed to fall in perfect alignment. He was a true gentleman; always opening doors, paying for our dates, and calling to say good morning or good night. He sends me text messages throughout the day. He even introduced me to some of his friends. Clearly, he has a long-term agenda. That other stuff might have still happened, but if I was just a side chick or flavor of the week I would have never met his friends. This must be getting serious.

Tonight, we're having a candlelight dinner at my place. We're both big on seafood so I'm making us shrimp alfredo, crab legs, and lobster tail. Everything smelled delicious and looked even better. I was ready to dig in, but first I had to get dressed. Darren would be here in less than an hour and I still had to shower and change.

I timed everything just right. The doorbell rang just as I was putting in my last earring. Taking one last look in the mirror, I admired how thick and tasty I looked tonight. Hopefully he will have the same sentiments.

He gave me a tight hug when I opened the door to let him in. The feeling of his body pressed up against mine was an indication of how this night would end.

"It's good to see you again, beautiful." He said warmly.
"Same to you, handsome."

I escorted him into the dining room where our seafood spread awaited us.

"Wow!" He said astonished. "Looks like you put your foot in this food!"

"I have a few skills." I said, proud of my accomplishment. "Have a seat. Let me fix your plate."

I was stepping into wife mode full throttle. His dinner plate was adorned with pasta filled with big, juicy shrimp, a lobster tail, and five king crab legs. If he couldn't see how much I was trying to impress him after tonight, then there is no hope for us. Not that it would be a problem. If there's one thing I know how to do its feed a man. I have yet to lose someone because he was malnourished - physically or sexually.

"Damn, girl! You tryin' to get a brotha' fat!?" His slang talk was so cute.

"Eat up!"

I handed him a crab zipper and crab cracker to go to work. I told you I am serious about my seafood. Once we were both settled with our dinner it was time to eat. Normally there would be light chatter between us, but not tonight. Either he was really enjoying his meal, or he wasn't alive - and I could see him moving. I'd catch him looking up at me and smiling here and there. I don't think he was aware that I saw him. Instead I kept enjoying my meal, anticipating my thank you that was sure to come.

Darren ate two plates full and cleaned both of them. My mission was accomplished. He enjoyed his dinner and now it was time to chill. After throwing back two shots of Patron and some mints we went to sit in the living room, taking the bottle with us. Within an hour the bottle was gone, we were feeling good, and he was feeling on me.

"Thank you for dinner, baby." Darren said as he started to nibble on my neck.

"You're welcome."

"Do you have any dessert?"

He pulled back and looked at me intensely. I knew exactly what he meant, and yes, I did have dessert for him. I leaned back into the couch in anticipation.

"I'll take that as a yes." He said, as he began to lift my shirt, exposing my breasts. "Nice and perky. Just how I like them."

Not another word was said. He began to gently grace his tongue around my areole, purposely teasing me to make my nipples rise. My eyes rolled in the back of my head. This was the moment I had been waiting for; at least I hope it was. Darren had a fetish for foreplay, but we never got past having oral sex. For a while it was good enough for me. I would just call up JD or Zack, my white chocolate drops, to finish what Darren started. But now feelings were getting involved. That was usually a red zone with me. I don't know why it's different with him, but it is. I'm praying that tonight we take it all the way to home base.

I must admit, Darren has a way of going the extra mile when he gets into his zone. It almost makes you not even want to have sex…almost. I was used to the licking, the sucking, and the finger fucking. I wanted more. I needed more. And I made damn sure to let him know just that.

"Fuck this!" I said as I wrapped my legs around him and flipped him over. "I want you now!"

Strangely, a look of fear overshadowed his face. For a split second it startled me. Then I felt his erection go down. What in the hell is going on? I've never had a man get soft on me. Is this dude gay or something? He pushed me off him and bolted for the door; pulling his pants up while running to get in his car. I tried to catch him, but he sped off. I stood at the door baffled and bewildered.

"What the fuck just happened?"

My ego was hurt. That was something I have never experienced before. At that very moment I decided I would never experience it again. Now I was standing at the door, horny as hell, and my dick bolted on me. Guess there was only one thing left to do at this point. I went to get my cell phone and scrolled down until the numbers slowed down. My options were Jordan, Josiah, Juan, Julian, or Justin.

Eenie meenie miney mo
Catch a penis, fuck it slow

If he hollers, go down low
Juan's the one I want to blow

I sent out my trademark 911-69 code via text. Within thirty seconds I got a reply.

Be there in 10

I guess this night wouldn't be a bust after all.

Gainell

Jamison Andrews was our latest business target. His technology company has an estimated net worth of around $17.4 Million dollars. If he hires us to do his external auditing and compliance for his finance department that would put us ahead of all our competitors. It would also include a nice bonus check for me, and I get to set the amount.

I spent all week wining and dining this prospect - as a business expense, of course. This included a lavish dinner for him and his top executives, a round of golf at the Windham Estates Private Golf Club, and several treats sent to his downtown office. I tried to keep business talk light, but I was starting to feel like now he was just milking us for all he could. That's not going to happen. I'm not spending another dime until I get his signature on the line.

"Mr. Andrews," I said, "this has been a wonderful week getting to know you and your staff better."

"Why thank you." he said in a cynical tone.

"Have you made your decision regarding our services? I believe you have all the information you need to come to an intelligent conclusion."

I pulled out the reverse psychology card. Of course, he was going to choose us. To do otherwise would suggest his intelligence wasn't up to par. He knew the move I was pulling - all the top executives and CEO's do it. And just like the rest of them he fell for it, but on his terms.

"Miss Moreau, let's be honest. You're only interested in the returns my business can bring you. Am I correct?"

"To be frank, yes."

Jamison sat back as if he expected me to give him a watered down answer. That's not how I do business. He needs to know that from the door.

"Interesting." He continued. "You are very up-front and direct."

"That's the only way I know how to be." I said. "Now it's time for you to make a decision. While we'd love to have your account on the books, and we've already proven how we can save your company millions, there are two things we are not about waste around here: and that's time and money. Do we want the returns? Yes. Will we earn them? Yes, we will earn every penny and more. That's what you wanted, am I correct?"

"Yes."

"So what is your answer? Are you ready to sign with AccuTron?"

I loved playing hardball with strong, powerful men. It gave me a rush to show them that I meant business. Tight suit, big breasts, and gorgeous hair aside, I needed an answer and I needed it now.

"Miss Moreau, you have yourself a new client."

"Welcome aboard. I promise you won't be disappointed."

I extended my hand to shake his in agreement. Half an hour later the paperwork was signed and everything was official. We would begin our operations with his company next month. The only thing left to do was receive payment. That would be done when his finance department processed their own paperwork which he said should take no longer than a week. For his sake I hope not. I want my money now.

Once he left the office I sat back and opened my special bottle of Moscato.

"To you, Nelli, for once again playing hardball…and winning!"

I took a sip of the fine wine and imagined the many ways I would spend my bonus check. My twin and I were well overdue for a vacation, and since our mother wanted to return to Italy I think it would only be fitting if we took her there in style. I called my mother to see how far along she got with the plans. She said nothing was set in stone yet.

"Don't worry about it, *Madre*. I'll take care of everything. This time next month you'll be gliding down the canals of Venice in a gondola with a crooning suitor there to grant your every wish!"

"You must have signed a new client." She said. "Congratulations!"

I laughed at how well she knew me. The rest of the day was spent going back and forth with my mother, GiGi, and the travel agent. By the end of the day everything was set. After a week of hard work to secure a cocky, arrogant client I deserve two weeks in Venice with my family.

GiGi met me for a celebratory dinner at our favorite Italian restaurant. There isn't a restaurant in America that does Italian food any justice, but this one comes close. It's owned by three generations of Italians, but with each generation came a little Americanization. The food is still amazing and the staff is friendly. They really know how to make their patrons feel special.

"Are the lovely *signores* ready to order?" Mario, our waiter, asked us.

"Si, signore." Nellie replied.

Nelli ordered the Rissoto with Shrimp and Zucchini. I wanted something lighter, so I ordered the Winter Minestrone soup. We'd top it off with an Italian Spritz punch and a slice of tiramisu cake and vanilla gelato.

Mario went to submit our orders. As we waited for our meal I filled GiGi in on the travel details. Our intentions seemed to be in sync as she was looking for a reason to get away as well.

"I think this is a great idea, Nelli!" She said. "We can certainly use the getaway from work and all the drama in the group."

"Please don't remind me!" I begged.

"Yeah, you're right. Let them two fight to the death."

"Girl, they already did that!"

"What are you talking about?" GiGi sat back, shocked, but not surprised.

"Phoenix and Emerald went head to head over a week ago. I thought you knew."

"I thought they just had a really bad argument. I didn't know they went to blows. They are so fu…"

I stopped her before she let the expletive slip. This was not the environment for such language, or such a conversation.

"GiGi, let it go. It's not even worth discussing anymore."

"You're right."

We quickly switched the conversation back to our visit to Italy. GiGi said she has been in contact with some of our family members and they've agreed to help make the transition for my mother as smooth as possible. After all, she's lived in America for over 60 years. A lot has changed about Venice since she left. Visiting for a month or two is one thing. Moving back on a permanent basis is something else.

"Do you know if mom will renounce her citizenship here?" GiGi asked.

"I don't think so." I said, as our meals arrived. "She didn't say anything about it."

Mario and another waiter placed our meals in front of us. Everything looked absolutely delicious.

"*Grazie.*" We both said in unison.

"*Siete i benvenuti! Buon appetite!*"

Summer

"Summer, when are you coming back to church?"

"Oh, mom. Not now."

My mother lays these guilt trips on me constantly. That's why I barely talk to her. She doesn't seem to understand that I have my own belief system and it differs from hers. I've tried to explain this to her many times, but my reasons keep falling on deaf ears. Yet I know better than to tell her I'm going to do something and not follow through. I will never hear the end of it.

"The sisters miss you, honey." She continues. "The pastor and first lady have been asking about you. They say you have a bright mind and a mission to fulfill, but you need to be in the House of the Lord in order to do it."

I can't argue with that point. Not because I believed it, but because I know that's her belief and you can't change someone's belief. Only they can do that for themselves. Out of respect for my mother I always listened to her. She strongly believed that by me returning to church my life would take a turn for the better. Maybe she was right, but if that's the case why did it turn for the worse when I was already in church?

For years I used to pray and ask God what happened in my life that caused such a drastic turning point. I used to be a go hard, faithful believer of God. The trinity was what I stood for and I would quote down anyone that tried to persuade me to believe otherwise. Their beliefs and gods meant nothing to me because I knew the Father, the Son, and the Holy Ghost always had my back.

Or so I thought.

Then in the sickest event my life turned upside down and inside out all in a matter of twenty-four hours. It was March 28, 2005, the day after Easter Sunday. I was renewed in the spirit and filled with gratitude and appreciation for my life and everyone in it. Everything was fine until my alarm went off. The song I had my alarm set to still sends shivers down my spine.

The day started off as any other. I got up, took a shower, and got ready for work. I walked into my job at Quest Logistics where I worked on the sixth floor as a customer service representative. It had nothing to do with traveling and speaking to the world - my greatest passion - but at that time it was what paid the bills. Before I got settled at my desk the manager at the time called me and seven other co-workers into his office. In no uncertain terms he handed us our pink slips and told us we had ten minutes to pack up and get out.

Always one to see the silver lining in every cloud I left without protest, which is more than I can say for the other seven unlucky individuals. I went to my desk, packed up my three photo frames and drink cup in my purse, and walked out the door with no intentions of looking back. I didn't say goodbye to anyone or exchange information to keep in touch. I had my fill of this place and everyone in it.

When I went to my car someone had side swiped me. *It's going to be one of those days!* With that thought I made a beeline home, got in my pajamas, and went to bed. No sense in tempting fate. But even as I rested in my footies and numbed out my sorrows with reality television my life was still falling apart without my permission.

The biggest blow was the phone call I got from my mother.

"Hey, mom." I said, trying to hide my depression.

"Sweetie, are you sitting down?"

"I'm actually lying down. Why? What's wrong?"

"I have some bad news. I hate to tell you this, but Latresha was found dead this morning."

Nothing else she said registered in my mind. Latresha was by far my favorite cousin. We had plans to travel the world, speaking to millions of women and making millions of dollars together. While I got sidetracked by taking on the job I just got fired from, she continued to hit the pavement, taking every speaking opportunity that came her way. She was finally building a reputation for herself. Her plan was to continue to work her connections and bring me in when I got ready.

That was going to be my game plan for tomorrow. I wanted to reach out to her and let her know it was time for me to get out there with her. I had nothing to lose and no reason to stay. My job just laid me off, I was in the last month of my lease, and I had no one or nothing tying me down. It was the perfect time to get started.

While her death was heartbreaking enough it's the way she died that killed my spirit. She did a conference a few months ago and afterwards met with a woman one-on-one. This woman was a mess; her husband of 13 years left her and their special needs child, she had no money or working experience so the best employment she could get was at a fast food restaurant. Her family had disowned her for marrying outside of her race. Even after their divorce they used that to further their own prejudices and refused to recognize her or her daughter. She was on the verge of suicide and came to my cousin for help.

Latresha started working with her. For a few weeks she was making progress. This woman got to a point where she thought she had everything under control and ended the sessions with my cousin. She was grateful for Latresha's guidance and for getting her back on the right track. Latresha hadn't heard from her since.

Then two weeks ago she was on a panel with a group of experts discussing the perils of single parenting. The panel had a four hour discussion talking about everything from dating to finance to childcare. After the panel discussion was over and everyone began to depart she was approached by a strange woman. Most of her head was covered with the hood on her jacket. From what Latresha could see this woman looked battered and beaten up by life.

"Ma'am, are you okay?" Latresha asked.

The woman took the hood off her head. It was the same woman she had helped years ago. She was stunned; what happened to her? The last time they spoke she had a better job, was finally dating again, and her child was doing well. This couldn't be the same woman, could it?

"You ruined my life." The woman said sternly. "Everything you taught me, everything you preached about was all a lie. I hope you burn in hell."

After that, Latresha began receiving a series of harassing emails, phone calls, and threatening letters at her home and office. Her reputation within the speaking community, the same reputation she worked so hard to build, began to fall apart. While other speakers said they supported her and could understand what she was going through, the organizations these speakers operated were not hiring her to speak anymore. Within a few weeks she went from being one of the most sought out motivators to one of the industry's tainted gurus.

The stress and uncertainty about the future of her career began to weigh on her. She had no one to talk to except for me, and even my words weren't strong enough to pull her through this. Looking back, maybe that's another reason why I gave up speaking and motivating. I couldn't even help my cousin who was also my best friend. How could I help a stranger?

One day she didn't show up to her office. Her assistant, Patty, had been calling her all morning. There was no response. Fearing the worse, she went to her condo to check on her. After knocking a few times and getting no response she used her key, praying she wouldn't come up on her boss' dead body. She searched every room; they were all empty. There was a sigh of relief immediately tailgated by a sense of fear and urgency. If she's not here, then where is she?

Inside, Patty knew something wasn't right, but she didn't want to cause a big media stir by filing a false missing person report with the police. She tried to call, text, and email Latresha again, this time showing her concern. The next day she went into work praying either for her boss to be in the office or for a response. She got a response, but it wasn't what she expected.

> *Dearest Patricia,*
> *I thank you for your years of dedication, devotion to the company and the cause, and most importantly our friendship. It means so much to me that even as the world has turned its back on me you still have my back. I pray that we meet again on the other side. I love you. I appreciate you. I thank you.*
> *With sincere gratitude,*
> *Latresha S. Miller*

Her body was found a few days later in a resort in Colorado. The mountains always gave her life. This time, they gave her death. The medical examiner did a thorough autopsy, but they never could rule on how she really died. On her death certificate it's listed as an unexplained death because while she tried to overdose on acetaminophen the units were no strong enough to even make her nauseous. She had no other health problems, no drugs were found in her system, and there were no signs of foul play. To the state her death remains a mystery. To me, I know her own internal guilt is what really killed her.

I haven't had the desire to speak or motivate anyone since that day. In fact, in that exact moment my mother delivered the news to me I lost all ambition for life. Gratitude be damned, the Universe, God, everything and everyone at that moment was against me. Instead of flying high and being a target, I sunk low and flew under the radar. Then I walked under the radar. Then I slithered under the radar until I finally just stopped.

While it may seem like I'm okay on the outside, my cousin's death still affects me to this day. I can still see that lady in my mind's eye - even though I never met her a day in my life. I could hear the tension and disappointment in her voice. I could sense the fire in her spirit that was thirsty for blood. I could also understand the cowardice of my cousin.

It's hard to accept the fact that there was someone you couldn't help, but what she should have realized is that not everyone can be reached. Some people don't want to be helped and some people expect you to do all the work. Her desire to change people's lives cost her own life, and not in a heroic way. I can't take that same chance. She was smarter than me, more knowledgeable than me, and stronger than me. If that one woman's antics caused her to go over the edge, I couldn't begin to imagine what it would have done to me. It's easier for me to play it safe and for the past eight years that's what I've been doing.

There are no ups and downs in my life. Everything moves along a flat line. I don't get hype about anything and I don't get disappointed. It all leads to the same inevitable fate - death - so why bother? My days and weeks are sickeningly predictable. I get up, go to work, come home, watch television, go to bed, and do it all over again the next day. On the weekends, I generally hang out with the girls, some random dude, or sulk in my own self-pity in my apartment.

It works for me. The girls have gotten used to it as well. They used to try tirelessly to motivate me again, but nothing ever worked. I can't do it because I'm too scared. I don't want to end up taking my own life like Latresha. I'd rather live a long, monotonous life than a purposeful, but possibly short, life. To each his own I say. After years of rebutting they finally got the message. Now I only get invites to do things sporadically. It kind of hurts that they discount me, but it also prevents me from having to say no. Still, some of those events sound fun, and they don't have anything to do with work. I could do those. Maybe I should say something to them. Maybe one day I will.

Giuseppina

Another satisfied client has so graciously rewarded my services with a lavish dinner at one of the finest restaurants in town. He spared no expense as my management staff and I were treated to whatever our hearts desired on the menu. We have been in partnership with this client for well over five years and every year the rewards for our services increase. We certainly earn the treatment and these anniversary dinners confirm it.

"A toast," I began, "to five years of growing commitment to excellence, innovation, and synchronicity with Advent Technologies."

"Cheers!" Everyone said in agreement. As the glasses around the table clanged repeatedly, I took a sip of my champagne, looking over everyone as a proud mother looks at her children when they celebrate yet another birthday. The food arrived and everyone enjoyed their meal. There were so many delicious choices on the menu, but I opted to keep it light. I have an image to maintain as their leader. The last thing they need to see is me ravaging through plate after plate of peach glazed salmon. One serving was enough. I'll have my indulgence tonight at home after dinner.

The dinner lasted for about two hours. When we departed, I stayed a little while longer, ensuring I was the last one at the restaurant in our group. It wasn't hard to do because everyone began to exit as it was getting late. Twenty minutes before the restaurant closed, I was finally alone and able to indulge freely. Mr. Langston, the owner of Advent and our gracious host tonight, left the tab open for me to place a to go order.

My inner fat girl kicked in and ordered another serving of peach glazed salmon. In addition to that I also ordered shrimp linguini alfredo, stuffed peppers, chicken kabobs, and three slices of cake: chocolate death, lemon zing, and tiramisu.

To make myself feel not as fat I tossed in a large Caesar salad for good measure. The waiter asked me if some of the guests were meeting at my house later to continue the celebration. Clearly my order was too large to consist of just me. I appeased him and said they were. I was lying through my teeth, but what business was it of his?

A rush was put on my order and my dinner was ready for me right as they were letting out the last customers. They closed out Mr. Langston's tab for the night. One of the waiters helped me carry the orders out to my car. As I drove home the blended aromas were calling my name. I drove as quickly as I could so I could indulge in their sweet delicacy. When I arrived home, I unloaded every meal from the car in one trip. I didn't bother spreading the dinners out. One by one, bag by bag, I overdosed on my guilty pleasure not once showing any sign of regret.

All four meals and three desserts were consumed in under an hour. Once my cravings were satisfied, I made a mango daiquiri and went to go watch television for the rest of the night. Not even five minutes after sitting down did I pass out from over-consumption.

Whenever I have a food binge I always wake up a few hours later feeling nauseous. Guilt started to set in as I began to feel bad for overindulging. Tears began to flow from my eyes. It happened again; I succumbed to my weaker side, feeling like I needed to feed myself more than necessary. Taunting voices begin to fill my head. *You're so fat! How can you eat so much? Your chins are jiggling!*

My heart began to hurt. I turned up the volume on the television to drown the voices out, but they only got louder. Seeking an escape, I went for the bottle of vodka I kept stashed away in my freezer. Shot after shot I begged, pleaded, and commanded them to shut up. With each shot the taunts hurt more.

After the fifth shot I felt even worse than I did before. I went upstairs to my bedroom and took off my clothes. Standing in front of my mirror I saw the illusion of an overweight version of me. There were rolls, dimples, sagging skin, varicose veins, and unsightly discoloration from stretch marks. This wasn't my body. I was trapped inside of this monster created in my head and I wanted out.

I ran to the bathroom and began to purge myself of these inner thoughts. Through forced regurgitation I released every bad image, thought and comment inside of me in addition to the five shots of vodka and the meals I consumed a few hours prior. The porcelain throne became my friend and foe in one sitting. When it was all said and done, I was completely emptied out. Nothing remained inside of me except tears, fear, and the sickening urge to do it again.

Phoenix

Today was my first time back at the gym since I had that fight with what's her name. I've been so busy with keeping myself preoccupied and distancing myself from her. This was one place I knew she would be. My only hope is that I don't run into her. It was early, like six in the morning, so there was a good chance I could get a good workout in and leave before it got busy.

I'm used to coming late at night so none of my usual workout buddies are here. One good thing about being here so early, outside of avoiding that ex-friend of mine, is I also get to avoid Myron. He is the classic definition of thirsty. I mean, the brother tries too hard to get my attention. No one grunts that hard when lifting weights. I could always tell when he was doing it intentionally because he would wait until I was watching to start. When I wasn't paying attention, or he thought I wasn't paying attention, he'd do them normally.

The kicker was he'd risk his own safety to try and impress me by putting on heavier weights to push himself. That was the story he always shared with me at the juice bar. I'll rightfully admit that sometimes I did flirt back innocently, but I never had any intentions on taking it anywhere. At least not to the level he was hoping to go. Although he never directly said anything, I could tell he wanted more than I was willing to give. Nevertheless, he was sweet and freely spent money on me at the juice bar so it was worth it.

I did a quick 45-minute workout before hitting the showers. By seven, I was dressed and ready to go. As I headed out to my car I noticed a familiar vehicle. My stomach started turning in knots. A few seconds after the car parked I could see Myron. I thought him up, and believe me that was not my intention. I'll be nice and give him some light conversation. Nothing more, nothing less.

As I walked towards the direction of his car I played it off like I was paying attention to my phone. I could feel him staring me up and down. A sly smirk came across my lips; I enjoyed moments like this. Any second now he would reach out for me. He was so close I could smell his cologne. I must admit, he smelled good. *Brace yourself girl. Here it goes.*

Myron walked right passed me and didn't say a word. Maybe he didn't see me. Before I could talk myself out of it, I yelled out his name.

"Hey, Myron."

He turned around as if to see who was calling him. Is he seriously going to act like he didn't see me?

"Oh, hey."

That was his only response before he turned around and continued to walk into the gym. Did he just brush me off like that? Something must be wrong. He's never played me off. If anything, I would have been the one to say hi and walked away. He must have been talking to that girl. Let me go in here and see what he knows. The last thing I need is a gym full of people assuming shit about me.

I started to go after him then stopped five hundred feet shy of the door. *This is stupid, Phoenix!* A displaced laugh escaped my lips. It was too early for the nonsense and I still had to go home and get ready for work. I'm sure our paths will cross again. If it happens a second time, then I'll see what's up. For now, I'll chalk it up to him being too nervous to stop and speak to me. Yeah, that's it. Poor guy is so twisted he can't even function. I guess that's what happens when you got it like that.

He walked right passed me.

This thought consumed my entire day to the point I could not focus on anything. Why was it bothering me so much? I didn't want to talk to him anyway, so what does it matter if he walked right passed me? He obviously wasn't angry with me; after all he did turn around and speak when I called his name.

I called his name.

Why did I do that? Did I want him to see me? The more I thought about it the more it drove me closer to the brink of insanity. By the end of the day I was writing out those two comments on paper. Five o'clock could not come fast enough. I needed a drink…fast! Something hard and stiff would do the trick.

Like Myron?

Where in the hell did that thought come from? It's official; I have lost my mind. As soon as my shift ended, I shut the computer down and made a beeline to the door. I didn't wait for everything to power down properly. I.T. can handle that in the morning. This morning's events were on repeat in my head. I sped home to get to my stash; I've never been so eager to have a drink in my life. Rush hour be damned, this was no time to sit in bumper to bumper traffic. I took the street way home. It's a little longer, but the highway was a parking lot and I needed that drink now.

When I got home, the first thing I did was reach for my shot glass and bottle of Absolut. I took two shots back to back and mixed a third with some cola. In a few minutes this morning's events will be far from my psyche and I can laugh this whole thing off. Sitting on the edge of my bed I waited for that moment to come.

Alcohol has a funny way of bringing things to the surface that one would never think existed within them. Instead of blocking out what happened with Myron this morning I started beating myself up mentally for not going after him. The opportunity was right in front of me and I let it slip. It really bothered me that he didn't stop to talk to me. It bothered me more that he didn't even initially stop in the first place. I know I wasn't losing my appeal in general, but could I be losing my appeal with him?

I lay back in my bed and played out that scenario over and over in my head. One time he stopped me and we talked. Thoughts of his flirtatious smile warmed my heart. In another thought I went to him. We shared a mango citrus smoothie, his treat, and talked about our plans for the day. Funny thing about both visions is that he didn't have on his wedding ring in neither one of them.

Why is it that after all these years I'm just now feeling him? Or this some sort of delusion created by the recent mercury retrograde? Yeah, that's it! It's my mental response to the intergalactic laziness of my ruling planet, Mercury. Astrology saves my ass yet again. There was no other rhyme or reason to feel the way I was feeling. My thoughts were being misconstrued; my reality tainted by a horrific image created to distract me.

A few hours passed by as I slip into an alcohol induced slumber. I woke up to nothing but a splitting headache. That was better than the other thoughts plaguing my mind. I took a couple of aspirin and went to make dinner. The remainder of my night was peaceful. Most of my thoughts were of their typical nature: anything that focused on or revolved around me. I liked those thoughts better anyway.

This was more my speed - watching mind numbing television with a glass of wine in one hand and my cell phone in the other. I could use some ego stroking to make me feel better. Let's get some other men activated in my mind. Better yet, let me activate myself in theirs.

Simultaneously I began holding a text conversation with five different guys. It didn't take long for my ego to feel loved and appreciated. I was even able to set plans for the weekend, and I'm not talking about your typical dinner and a movie. These plans required overnight packing, hotel reservations, and an American Express black card. That's the only way I know how to live.

As I began to wind down, thoughts of Myron slowly started to creep in again. Damn it, I thought we were done with this! I quickly shifted my thoughts back to my pending weekend plans, but they were no match to the image of his bulging muscles glistening with sweat as he does military style push-ups. Man, I'd love to be underneath all of that.

Get it together, Phoenix!

Emerald

Ever since our sexual encounter a few days ago Chauncey has been on me. He calls me every day, sometimes a few times a day, and flirts with me all the time at the gym. I try to keep it low key, but he's practically falling over himself whenever I'm there. It's cute though; I've never had a guy this into me so I'm not about to ruin it. If Phoenix could see how he reacts to me she would flip. She's used to being the only one getting attention. That holier-than-thou attitude makes her feel like she's a thousand times above everyone else. I used to joke around and tell her she was going to drown one of these days from having her nose so high up in the damn air. Now I was praying for it.

Someone who does know how to keep things low key and discreet is Myron. I've seen him twice since that night. Both times he tried to proposition me, but I resisted. That night was different. There was no one else around and I was on a mission for vengeance. In my mind, it's already been accomplished. I've already moved on to the next phase of my plan. He, on the other hand, has not.

It doesn't bother me, though. I like Myron and may actually take him up on that offer one night. Chauncey never did find out what happened before him. I guess Myron and I were thinking alike in that regards. The less people knew the better for the both of us.

Things in my life were starting to put themselves back in order. With Phoenix finally out of the picture I can focus on getting myself that BMW like Nelli or even snagging a good man like Wren. I already have Laila's sex life beat. When I told her about what happened at the gym she screeched with glee. What got her the most was when I told her about me smiling at Myron while riding the hell out of Chauncey.

"That's some shit I would have done!" She replied.

Man, I love my girls. I'm glad the canceled friendship didn't affect the whole group - at least on my end. As far as that other one, well, she got hers coming. All the dirt that I have on her is about to come right back. There were perks to being the one she told all her secrets to; well, perks for me. Knowing her she probably thought I either wasn't listening or forgot everything by now.

Not even a little bit!

These thoughts of future revenge were making me hot and horny. The gym is set to close in an hour. I think I need to do a late night workout. After getting dressed I headed over to the gym. When I arrived it was fifteen minutes past nine. I had just enough time to do my run on the treadmill. As soon as I walked in the door, I spotted Chauncey. Just the person I needed to see. I gave him my slick half smile - he knew what that meant - and headed to the women's locker room. After throwing on my shorts and tying my hair back I walked out to go to the treadmill. I was met at the entrance by yet another sweet surprise.

"Hey, Sweetness." Myron said, reaching out for a hug.

"Hey, you!" I replied, returning the love. "I didn't know you were here tonight."

"It was a last minute call."

"I see."

"I saw your girl the other day."

"My who?"

"Your friend, what's her name?"

I had to giggle. Either he was playing this off, or he seriously forgot her name…and I was not about to help him remember it.

"I'm sorry, boo, but I don't know who you're talking about."

"Oh well, it doesn't matter. Listen, I need to run, but I'd love to meet up for a smoothie. Will you be here Saturday afternoon?"

Saturday is the one day of the week when I work out before seven. I didn't really care for the gym's health treats for humans. The taste was disgusting; plus, it's just not my thing.

"Thanks, but I'll pass. I'm not really big on their juice bar."

"I understand. Well maybe I'll see you anyway." His cell phone rang. "I have to take this. Take care, beautiful."

He gave me a kiss on the lips and walked away. I guess there wouldn't be a replay of that event tonight. It didn't matter because I still had the main guy that I wanted and in less than an hour I would have him, and this entire gym, all to myself. I finally made it to the treadmill after being stopped by a couple more people. Now I only had half an hour to do my run. Going full throttle was not about to happen so I opted for an intense jog instead. It would still warm me up for what was about to commence. At this point that's all I could think about.

Wren

The drama between Jason and I had finally calmed down. He quit asking me questions, but stayed in touch with the police to see if they had any leads. They said when something came up they would be in touch, but we both knew his case was filed away, never to be looked at again. That was fine with me. Hopefully we won't have to walk this path again.

Even though he seized interrogating me I still felt like he suspected me of doing something. Sure, I did it, but he wasn't about to find out. Besides, I never did find out who that anonymous voice was in the background. The message is still in my voice mail as a reminder not to get too comfortable just yet. I have to stay on my toes in case he slips up again. The stress was getting to me. It's time for me to have some fun. I called up Laila to see what we could come up with for the girls. As soon as she answered I started ranting.

"I need a girl's night!"

She laughed on the other end of the line.

"Well hello to you, too, heifer!"

"Hey, girl!" I cleaned it up quick. "How are you? That's good. I need a girl's night!"

"I'm so done with you!" She giggled.

"I'm serious, La! Too much shit has happened in my life in the past few weeks and I need to regroup. What say you?"

"Shit, you know I'm down. Name the time and place, I'm there."

We decided to meet up at a restaurant instead of someone's house. That way we all could get out before the weather turned too cold. After a few suggestions we started to get the night together. We had one hell of a night planned for us. The only thing we had to figure out was how to mend the snag in the group.

"I guess we're all set!" Laila said excitedly. "So, what are we going to do about Phoe and Emma?"

"Oh, yeah." I thought about it for a minute. "I think it would be best if everyone gave their input. As for me, I want them both to be there, but if there's going to be drama then neither one should show up. I can't pick one over the other because I don't know the entire situation. That's not how I roll and you know that."

"I feel the same way." Laila said. "I know both sides and honestly they both fucked up. I can't side with one over the other, but if they can bury the hatchet for one night then I think it would be great for all of us to be able to hang out again. We haven't done that since we all met at your house over a month ago."

"I know. Well let's call the girls and see what they think about it. I'll call Nelli and you can call GiGi. We'll have one of them call Summer."

"Ready? Set? Go!" Laila said, and clicked over.

That girl was too crazy. I called Gainell on the other line. When she answered I connected our call back to Laila. She was able to get Giuseppina.

"What the hell happened now?" Gainell said after she heard all our voices.

"Damn, Nelli!" Laila said. "Why does it have to be drama?"

"It's not bad, Nelli." I said. "We've got something planned for all of us. Can one of y'all call Summer?"

"I'll call her." Giuseppina said and clicked over. She was back a few seconds later with Summer on the line.

"Hey, Summer!" We all said practically in unison.

"Is this an intervention?" She asked. "What did I do now?"

"Look," I said, "I'm going to need you heifers to be a little more positive with your outlook! Okay, here's the deal."

Laila and I proceeded to explain our plans for girl's night. The girls were excited to finally have a night out. Gainell and Giuseppina were scheduled to fly out a couple of days after so it would be a good time to see them before they depart to Italy. The only thing that remained was in inevitable question: should we invite Phoenix, Emerald, both, or neither.

"Well here's what I think." Gainell said. "If they can act like adults then there's really no reason to pick one over the other. If they can't then the last thing I need is some immature bitches killing my vibe."

"Well damn, Nelli!" Giuseppina said. "Tell us how you really feel."

"Shut up!" Nelli said.

"I agree with my other half. If they're cool, I'm cool. If not, then there's no need for them to come."

"What about you, Summer?" I asked. "What do you think?"

"Why does it matter?" Summer asked. "They're going to do what they want regardless, so let's just go and see what happens."

"Your nonchalant ass would say something like that." Gainell retorted.

"But am I wrong?" Summer responded.

"She's right, Nelli." Laila said. "Let's just put the offer out there and see who says what. Twenty bucks says Phoenix will show up to claim her spot and piss Emma off."

"I see your twenty and raise you fifty." Giuseppina said. "Emma's not going to let her get all of us. Not without another fight."

"Ladies! Ladies!" I yelled, trying not to bust a gut from laughing. "We are not betting on our friends. Besides, I got a Ben that says neither one of them will show up."

"Y'all are a mess!" Gainell said. "I'm staying out of this. Just slide me the money. I'll hold it."

"Well, it's settled." Laila said. "We'll invite them both with a disclaimer. Whoever shows up, shows up. Agreed?"

We all agreed.

Shortly after, we all began to depart from the conversation. Laila volunteered to extend the invitation to Emerald and Phoenix. Laila and I were the last ones to hang up the phone. Jason walked in a few seconds later. He looked like he just lost his best friend.

"What's wrong, baby?" I asked.

"They found my car. It was in a fucking lake! How did my car get into a fucking lake, Wren?!"

My heart dropped. Was he asking me out of curiosity, or was he accusing me? I had to play this one smooth so I wouldn't blow my cover.

"Wait, what? How did they find it in a lake?"

"The complex it was in called the gas company because they saw oil in the lake. They thought there was a line leaking underground. When the gas company came out to inspect that's when they discovered my car."

"Damn, baby. I'm sorry to hear that."

He looked at me as if he wanted to say something, but he decided against it. Personally, I think it's a damn shame that this grown ass man is in tears over a hunk of metal. The car meant something to him, but that's why I had to do what I did. He didn't have the same regard for me as he did for his car. Maybe now that I broke him down he'll be a little more sensitive to my needs. My mission has been accomplished.

Laila

"Hell no!" Emerald screamed in my ear. "You couldn't pay me to be in the same room with that bitch, Laila."

"Look, Emma, we're not asking you two to be besties again. Wren wants to have girl's night with ALL of us! That means you AND Phoenix. You can't put aside your differences for a few hours? You don't even have to stay the entire time if you don't feel comfortable."

Emerald was silent on the other end. This was some straight up nonsense. How can this grown woman in her mid-thirties be so childish and vindictive? Discrepancy be damned, she can pull herself together for one night. If not for us, then at least for Wren. After all she's done for Emerald she owes her one. She finally replied.

"Look, I can't promise anything, but I will think about it."

"That's all I'm asking you to do. Besides, I haven't seen you in so long. I'd hate to miss an opportunity to catch up girl style because of this. It's your call, but I do hope you come."

"Thanks, Laila. I'll give you a call by this weekend to let you know."

"Okay. Seriously, Emma. Come!"

"I said I'll think about it."

"Don't think…do!"

"Bye!"

I could hear her snickering before she hung up. She thought I was playing, but I was dead serious. Well I had one phone call out of my hair. It was time to wrestle with the other one. Normally, Phoenix is the understanding one. This, however, might change her tune. Only time will tell. I dialed her number.

"Hey, chick!" She said, answering the phone.

"Hey! I got an invitation for you."

"Cool. For what?"

"Wren wants to have a girl's night next weekend. Are you down?"

"Why in the hell would you ask me that?" She laughed. "Of course I'm down!"

"I knew you would be, but there's a catch. She wants us ALL to be there."

"Okay, and…"

"That includes Emma."

"Who?"

"Don't play with me, Phoenix! You know who I'm talking about."

"No, I'm sorry, but I don't."

Is this chick really going to act like she doesn't know who Emerald is? It was cute the first couple of times she played that off; even kind of funny. Now it was just annoying as fuck.

"Look, save that game for someone else. Are you coming or not?"

"I'll be there. There's no reason why I shouldn't be."

"Okay, I'll let Wren know."

"Wait, you can't invite me to girl's night and not tell me what kind of debauchery we're going to get into. I need details!"

Now that was my Phoenix. I laughed at her as I gave her the tentative itinerary. She was more than happy to be in attendance. See, if I could get this type of attitude from Emerald this would be perfect. That might be asking for too much though. I'll take what I can get.

"Alright chick, I have to go." Phoenix said. "Call me if you guys need help with anything."

"Roger that, chica!"

With that we ended our conversation. I called Wren with an update. She had just got off the phone with Emerald.

"What did she tell you?" I asked.

"Probably the same thing she told you, that she would think about it and let me know."

"Figures."

"What did Phoenix say when you asked her?"

"She's fired up and ready to go!" I laughed, thinking about her reaction.

"So Emma being there won't be a problem?"

"See, that's the thing, Wren. She's still on this amnesia kick of hers. Every time I mentioned Emma she acted like she didn't know who I was talking about."

"Really? She's still on that?"

"Yeah, but I don't think she's playing. You know how Phoenix can be. When she dismisses someone she really will forget who they are."

"Do you really think she can do that shit though, Laila? Like, forget them for real?"

"I think so. I mean everything in life is mental; it's all about your thought processes and how you react to things. Maybe she really was so close to the edge that she pushed Emma out of her memory for good."

"But why would she do that?"

"Because Emma can be a bitch sometimes, Wren, and you know that."

"Yeah, but…"

"But what?"

Wren was silent for a second. She tried to come up with an excuse for Emerald. We all have. Just like every other time she was unsuccessful.

"I've got nothing."

"We never do!'

"Well, let's just have a great night and pray everyone meshes well again."

"Yeah, we'll need to pray hard on this one."

I spoke with Wren for a few minutes more before she had to go. These bitches had me stressed out. Sometimes I wonder why so many women choose to have male friends over females. Then we go through shit like this and it becomes crystal clear. But I love my girls, all their crazy asses, and wouldn't trade them for the world. Right now though, I need one of my male friends in my presence. I wasn't in the mood to fuck; I just wanted to talk. Chuck's always good for that, and if I change my mind he'll be good for a fuck, too.

Summary

The alarm went off in my room for fifteen minutes straight. I didn't even have the strength to hit the snooze button. Today my spirit was heavy. Nothing in my life reflected anything I envisioned five years ago. There was nothing special about the day; just another constant reminder that I'm not where I want to be…wherever that is.

The desires have been plentiful: cosmetologist, fashion designer, actress, model, motivational speaker. I was never short on options for a career choice. What I did lack was desire, know-how, and self-confidence. That's why they all remained visions and became nothing more. The dream that had the most potential of becoming a reality was becoming a motivational speaker. I turned that dream into a goal after going to one of those empowerment seminars. You know, the ones that get you all hyped up about changing your life. I was on fire for about a month. After that, the desire started to dwindle. I didn't want to lose that spark though. I finally found something worth fighting for and wanted to make it happen. When I found out Latresha was trying to do the same thing we teamed up to be each other's accountability partner.

Latresha was way more successful at follow through than me. For years she built up her reputation while I watched and waited on the sidelines. What was I waiting for? I still don't know to this day. All I know is that when I got the call she took her own life that dream was buried for good. No amount of excavation would revive it. I'm fine with that. What I'm not okay with is feeling lost, but since I have nowhere else to go I just wait. Sit…and wait.

The aura of depression and disappointment were heavy in the room. Paralyzed with indecision, I have once again become its victim. Why is it so difficult for me to figure out what I want to do? Why can't I decide what makes me happy? What does it feel like to be happy?

My head started to spin. It was time to nip this feeling in the bud before it became too strong. I popped a couple of "Special K" pills that I got from one of Laila's dudes. After chasing them with a shot of vodka and ginger ale I rolled over, closed my eyes, and waited for the dancing butterflies to greet me in my dreams.

"Summer!" I heard a sweet, energetic voice say my name. "Get up, honey! We've got work to do!"

I opened my eyes and was no longer in my bedroom. When I sat up my body was sprawled across a hammock gently swaying in the wind. Palm trees, white sand, and bright blue skies surrounded me. A pretty pink and yellow drink with an umbrella in it sat on the table next to me. *I have no clue where I am, but I'll take it.*

"Summer! We have to get ready!"

I looked back to hear where the voice was coming from. A young woman was just turning away from the door and walked back into the beach house. *Where am I?* I began to wonder. *And who is she?*

"Who's in here?" I said as I walked in through the sliding glass door.

This was one exquisite looking beach house. The walls in the back were made of plexiglass; sturdy, but crystal clear. You could see a beautiful view of the waves gently flirting with the shores before them. The furniture pieces were bright and exciting; a candy red lounge chair sat adjacent to the cobalt blue love seat. Below them lay a plush white floor throw rug. Swirling colors of art pieces adorned the walls while photos of possible loved ones graced the tables.

This is a nice place! I wonder who lives her.

"There you are sleepy head!" I heard the voice say behind me.

It couldn't be.

I turned around to finally put a face to the voice that had caressed my ears. Either my eyes were playing tricks on me, or heaven had finally opened its doors because before me stood my best friend, my life blood, my muse…Latresha.

Tears welled up in my eyes. Was she really standing before me? If I reached out, could I touch her? Before I could construct another thought she had me in her arms, rocking me back and forth as if we hadn't seen each other in years. I guess it was fitting because we literally haven't communicated in that long. She pulled back and looked me up and down as if to examine how life has been treating me. Clearly she was also seeing an illusion because in her eyes nothing had changed.

"Girl, doesn't it feel wonderful to finally live out our dreams?" She asked.

"What?"

"I mean, look around us, Summer! We did it! We finally made it to the top!"

She squealed in delight as I stood there still baffled that she was even in my presence. Then it hit me. I must be dreaming…or dead. Did those pills kill me? She snapped me out of what surely would have been a string of questions.

"Okay, go put your bathing suit on and meet me by the beach for our planning session." Latresha said, followed by another squeal. "This is so exciting!"

She bounced out the door wearing a navy blue bikini and floppy sunhat. Finally, the tears dropped. I haven't felt like this in so long that it was scaring me. She was right; we had finally made it. I no longer care how I got here, but I hope I can stay here forever. Following her instructions, I walked to what must have been my room and changed into a mono-kini swimsuit. With my own oversized sunhat and Chanel shades I stepped out the glass doors and met her beachside, ready to participate in whatever she desired.

We were out there for what seemed like days. It was a hypnotizing moment. The weather was perfect. It wasn't too hot or too cold and there was just enough of a breeze to keep us comfortable without blowing our papers everywhere. Our drinks remained frozen and refreshing and the ideas for business growth kept flowing in abundance.

"It's so great to see you again, Latresha!" I said. "I really missed you."

"What are you talking about? I've been here the entire time."

"I mean, I missed you when I was at home. It's been a real struggle to stay motivated. Since you died, I can't…"

"Whoa, sweetie! What do you mean since I 'died'? What are you rambling about?"

Then it hit me. She has no clue she's dead. She's not in my world; I'm in hers. All of this was her vision and she brought me into it for a reason. I may not know a lot, but I know not to fuck up an angel's intermission when it happens. I retracted my statement with something more fruitful and positive. That is easier for me to do here than anywhere else.

"I meant since you left." I said with laughter. "Since you moved away it's been difficult."

"Girl, don't scare me like that! I thought I was a goner!" We both laughed together. "I understand, sweetie, but remember that your environment is everything. If you don't have a positive place to grow you need to create it!"

"I know. That's why I'm here with you. I need to find a way to create a better environment for myself because the one back home will surely kill me if I don't do something about it."

"Well then, let's get started. What do you want your environment to look like? Who do you want in it? How do you want it to make you feel? Details, girlie! I need details!"

I missed these talks Latresha and I used to have. It was so much easier to stay focused and on point when I had her in my life. Now my only support system needed to be taken with a glass of water and on the low. This energy she had with her pierced my soul and infused it with faith and hope for a brighter future. The burdens I carried before were no longer in existence. This is what I was missing. This is why I believe she brought me here. Now we were going to create a game plan to take back with me. Even from the other side she was still looking out for me.

"...and that's it!" She said, closing her notebook and preparing to go back inside.

"That's a lot!" I said. "What if I can't remember it all? What if I mess up somewhere? What if I get it wrong? What if..."

"What if...what if...what if...sweetie! You're missing the point! If all that stuff happens, so what? What matters is that you're trying and you're progressing. You will mess up. You will forget some of these things. You will get it wrong at times. And you will survive." She leaned down to give me a hug. "If you only have one take away from this entire beautiful day of ours let it be this: You are an ordained child of the Most High and no one nor nothing can stop you from having what has already been marked as yours. The only thing you need to do is believe, have faith, and move towards what you want. That's it. That's all."

"I love you, girlie!"

"I love you, too, sweetie!" A brisk wind blew across the water. "Ooh, it's time to go in!"

She started to run towards the beach house. Halfway, she turned around and yelled back.

"Remember what I said, sweetie, and you'll be wildly successful by your own definition. That's all that matters. Everything else is filler! I love you!"

With that, she ran inside and shut the door. I turned around in my chair, thinking about everything that just happened. My mind was oblivious to the tidal wave that approached me. She was right. The only thing that mattered in this entire equation was me. It was my job to secure my happiness and success, not anyone else. With that thought a smile graced my lips. She did it again.

"I'm ready, God. I really am."

A tidal wave crashed on me. Swimming in the sea of possibilities I crossed over from her world to mine with a new determination to create a better life for myself and those that I love.

Giuseppina

The stress was getting to me. Gainell and I only had a few days to get our mother prepared to move to Italy and I still had things to take care of personally. This new client of ours is driving me bat shit crazy! He has way too many demands, and most of them have nothing to do with his accounting needs. Things were getting out of hand. Before I leave town I must set him straight or he's going to drive my entire office off a cliff.

"Sandy, can you set up a meeting with Mr. Sandoval for this afternoon? Tell him it's important." I said, determined to set this guy straight once and for all.

"What if he's not available?"

"Then put him through to me."

While she worked on getting Mr. Sandoval on the line, I finished up a proposal for a new client that would replace him if he didn't get his act together. A few moments later my line buzzed. It was Sandy.

"Mr. Sandoval is demanding to speak with you."

"Demanding?" I asked. "Put him through."

I quickly ingested a handful of chocolate candies before he got on the line. I needed the chocolate to calm my nerves down. While I wasn't about to approach him with guns blazing, I was tired of walking on eggshells."

"Hello, Mr. Sandoval." I said, calming my nerves. "How are you today?"

"I was fine until your secretary demanded that I come in tomorrow. I think you need to have a talk with the help. She's apparently forgotten who's in charge here."

"Mr. Sandoval let's get one thing straight. My employees are the biggest asset to my company. With that said, please do not refer to them as "the help." This is not some 1800's plantation or third world country where the rich and powerful rule over the small and meek. We are all one big family here and as the leader of this family I will not let you belittle or berate anyone on my staff."

"Excuse me?"

"Which brings me to the purpose of why I had my wonderful *administrative assistant* call your office. Our contract, the one that I am holding in my hand, outlines services of weekly bookkeeping, monthly reports, quarterly audits, and yearly tax preparations. Nowhere in this contract did we ever mention extra services such as phone calls, contact connections, and dinner reservations that you, for some odd reason, think is our responsibility."

"I'm the client and…"

"Let me finish, Mr. Sandoval. We are an accounting firm, not a concierge service. If you need help with maintaining your email contacts then I suggest you get an email service provider. If you can't find out why your black card isn't working then you need to call your credit card company. Just because there's a financial element involved does not make it our problem. Consider this a verbal warning. Please stick to the services outlined in the contract. If this is not convenient for you then we can meet to either add an addendum or terminate the contract. It's your call."

Mr. Sandoval was outraged, as I expected.

"I have never been so disrespected in my life!"

"It's not disrespect, Mr. Sandoval. It's called running a business. Do we have a deal?"

Mr. Sandoval's line disconnected. I was a bit shaken up after the confrontation. Drama is not my strong suit, but I think I handled the situation well. Now I needed something to really calm my nerves. I reached in my desk for my emergency Trix and inhaled both cookie bars before it even had a chance to melt between my fingers. That hit the spot. I turned around in my chair and reached for my jug of chocolate milk. When I turned back Sandy was standing in the doorway with tears in her eyes.

"What's wrong, Sandy?" I asked. "Step inside and close the door behind you."

Sandy came in and sat in front of my desk.

"I'm going to apologize in advance for eavesdropping on your conversation with your client."

"No need to apologize, Sandy." I thought about what she said then let out a snicker. "Did you really just call him 'your client?' I guess he rubbed you the wrong way!"

Sandy always addressed everyone by their name, even when they were mean and nasty to her. It took a lot to get on Sandy's bad side. I think after all he's put her through Mr. Sandoval can safely take stock in that space.

"I apologize." Sandy said. "He just rubs me the wrong way. Anyway, I heard how you defended me, defended us all. It was nice of you to do that, Miss Moreau. I appreciate it and I'm sure everyone else does as well."

"Listen, Sandy, we are a family here. No one gets walked over; not on my watch. I meant what I said to Mr. Sandoval and if he can't handle it then he's more than welcome to find another firm that will let him treat people like trash. That may fly somewhere else, but definitely not here."

"You are awesome!" Sandy said. "That's why I love working here!"

"Well I'm glad you feel that way."

"Let me get back to work. I just wanted to say thanks for sticking up for us. You know we'd all do the same for you."

"I know, and thank you for all that you do around here. You truly are my right hand and I appreciate you more than you know."

She smiled and walked out the door, closing it behind her. She knows me so well. There are two things that always get to me: strong arguments and sappy moments. I just experienced them both within five minutes of each other. Screw a glass; I'm going to need the entire quart for this.

Gainell

"No the fuck he didn't!" I said in amazement.

As I sat and listened to my twin pour her heart out, I couldn't help but to become angry. I don't know this client of hers, but no one makes my sister feel that way. Granted she can get a tad close to her employees, she has a right. Most of them have been with her since she opened her business over ten years ago. Sandy helped her formalize everything, and for that jerk to belittle them in such a harsh tone made my blood boil. He probably dropped a few "n" bombs and "b" words after he hung up. He just seemed like the type. God have mercy on his soul if he did and may the Universe keep him as far away from me as possible.

"Listen, GiGi, you did the right thing." I said, trying to calm her down. "There's no need to go off the deep end with this. He's a jerk and karma has a special way of getting back at people like him. Don't worry what he said. Besides, you already have a better replacement ready for when he terminates the contract. Let go and be open to receiving someone bigger and better."

"You're right, sis. He just made me so mad! I had to take out an entire carton of Nesquik just to calm myself down."

"GiGi, no!" I screamed in her ear. "Don't do that to yourself! You know how you get when you're upset. You eat every damn thing in sight!"

The last thing I needed was for my sister to have another relapse and start binge eating again. She has a bad association with food: she uses it for everything. When she's celebrating she loads up on cake and ice cream. When she's horny or heated chocolate is her fix. When she's emotional she reaches for the candy. Anything financial sends her to the greasiest restaurants in town. For the past few weeks she's been good. Now this bastard done reactivated her second stomach. Son of a bitch!

My words were falling on deaf ears. My sister was knee deep in snack cakes by now. I could tell as her words went in and out while she was talking. It was disheartening to hear my sister backslide over an addiction she fought for so long to overcome. It took her years to even allow herself to admit she had a problem. She's been straight for the past couple of years. Now here comes this bastard pushing her over the edge. If she slips and falls that will be years of work down the drain. I can't let that happen to her.

"Listen, GiGi, you have got to pull it together."

"What do you mean?" She said with a muffled sound.

"You're doing it again. You're searching for comfort through food and it never works. I understand that you are upset, but don't do this to yourself again."

"Are you saying that I eat too much? Are you calling me fat?"

"No, sweetie! That's not what I'm saying at all."

"Then what are you saying?"

"I'm saying…"

I thought about it for a minute. Anything spoken after this point is sure to send her spiraling out of control. This was a delicate situation and could not be handled over the phone.

"I'm saying I'll see you in a few minutes."

Whoever this Mr. Sandoval character is better go into hiding because if he ever crosses my path I am going to straight kick his ass! This is some bullshit he is putting my sister through. Flying down the interstate I was trying to maintain my composure and not lost my cool. My sister is the sensitive half between us two and I am the protector. I guess it's because I'm the oldest. When someone or something affects her it automatically sends me into defense mode. That's where I'm at this very moment.

I pulled into a parking space and made a beeline for her office. Her door was closed but that didn't stop me. I barged in through the door just as she was downing yet another quart of chocolate milk. The poor thing was beside herself in grief and despair. The second she saw my face she went from barely keeping it together to completely falling apart.

"Sweetie," I said to her, reaching for the container, "put it down. It's not going to make any of this better."

She starts squealing in high pitched Italian. My twin has officially reached her breaking point. Sitting on her lap, I held her as she cried her eyes out. Sandy peaked in to see if we were okay. I waved my hand to motion her to close the door. I'm sure Sandy was a sweet woman, but this was a personal situation and she has no place here.

"It's okay, sweetie!" I said as she cried against my chest. "You did the right thing. You already have another client lined up and business is booming for you. There are other more deserving clients than that *cafonè*."

More squeals came from her lips. She was processing what I said. I know she wanted to rebuttal, it's in her nature to try to appease everyone, but I will not let her get away with it this time. As far as Mr. Sandoval, his days were numbered. The one thing you don't do is piss off an Italian. Pretty or not, rich or not, one way or another we will get your ass back. He's about to learn that lesson the hard way.

"Come on, sweetie. Pull yourself together so we can get out of here."

"I can't go now, Nelli. I have too much to do."

"Is it anything that will cause you to die today if you don't do it?"

She shook her head no. I gave her a few minutes to wrap everything up. I left her office to talk to Sandy. She was genuinely concerned about my sister. I can respect that and appreciated her for it. Without going into detail, I let her know she needed to leave early and placed Sandy in charge. It wasn't anything she's not already used to doing. There were only a few hours left in the workday. Most of the agents were out with clients anyway, so Sandy could hold down the fort until the end of the day. Once the orders were laid out, I went back into my sister's office. Somehow, she managed to find a hidden candy bar and was on the last few chews.

"What the fuck, GiGi!?"

I took a deep breath and grabbed her coat.

"Let's go before you kill yourself in here."

Phoenix

Three more days! I kept saying in my head. I could really use a break because everyone I came across was getting on my last nerve. I don't know why people think I'm obligated to do shit for them. None of these mother fuckers were there when I needed them. When I was sitting in my cold apartment after being laid off with no heat, no food, nothing, where in the fuck were they? Not giving a damn about me. For months I reached out to others and asked for help. I mean, why say you're there for me then turn your back when I need you? And people wonder why I stay to my fucking self.

Here's the situation. My cousin, Trina, just found out she's pregnant by some random dude - and yes, he's random because she doesn't even know who the father is. She got kicked out by my aunt because her husband wants to keep this image that they're some sort of fucking pristine family. I hate that bastard with a passion. Now she's pregnant, homeless, alone, and only fifteen years old. She came to me and asked if she could stay here until she turned sixteen in a couple of months. Then she plans to emancipate herself so she can be on her own.

Now this is the same chick that convinced her mother, my aunt, not to lend me money when I needed to pay my rent. Instead, she wanted the money to buy some $500 boots. Of course, my aunt put her daughter before me, and I was left to do some rather unethical things just to make sure I didn't get evicted. Isn't it funny how the tables have turned? Yeah, that bitch can go suck a dick for all I care. I don't care how old she is. She's not laying up in here!

That may be crude of me, but shit, so was how she played me. Before I went through my moment Trina and I were tight. She was like the baby sister I never had. I always had her back. When she was having problems with kids in her middle school bullying her, I snatched those little bitches up and gave them the business. To this day none of them will even look her way because they know I have a special spot for them in the woods if they fuck with her again. Well, I did until she played me.

As far as my aunt, that bitch can go to hell, to, right alongside her flaming ass husband. That fucker is more fabulous than your local department store's little girl's section. I don't know how she can't see it. Probably because she's so desperate to get some dick that she'll take it any way he gives it to her. From what I hear, it's not even coming straight from him, but some vibrator. How fucked up is it that your own husband won't stick his pole in your hole? He had to resort to a toy. That didn't send up any red flags? Dumb ass bitches.

I've had a hell of a week. The word *no* has spewed from my lips more times that I care to count. I need to take this feeling and use it for something better than stressing over these assholes. It's time for me to hit the gym. Plus, I could use some ego stroking from the local patrons. The gym would be open for a couple more hours. Let me go put this energy to good use.

The first hour at the gym was spent in hot yoga. I had to recondition my muscles to being stretched and worked out. It felt good to get my body acclimated to working out again. It was also a great stress reliever; I haven't felt this good in a while. When yoga class was over I went to do a few more stretches before starting my hour run on the treadmill.

While I was stretching I noticed Myron was on the lower level doing his workout. I could hear him straining to lift those weights. I watched him for a while to see if he was pushing himself to try and impress me again, and - of course - he was. Maybe I should go down there and give him a little motivation.

"Hey there!" I said, standing in front of his workout bench.

"Hey." He said without even looking up.

Was he really trying to play me like I wasn't standing here? He put down the barbell and finally looked up at me. Wiping the sweat off his brow he gave me a crooked smile. I never noticed he had a dimple. It was tiny, yet cute. Myron was actually very attractive. When I looked down I noticed his ring was off. Could he now be on the market? I guess now is as good a time as any to ask.

"So how are things going with you?" I asked.

"Good."

"How's the family?"

"Everyone's good. Listen, I got to finish my workout so I can get out of here. It was good to see you."

He stood up and walked towards the weight balls. Did he just blow me off? This was the second time I've seen him and he pushed me to the side. Fuck that! He wasn't that damn cute anyway. There's nothing worse than an arrogant man. I went back upstairs to claim my treadmill. I could still see him from where I was, but I refused to look down at him. Maybe look down on him, but not at him.

Ten minutes later I glanced over to see if he'd left yet. My eyes were on fire as I saw him hug my newest arch enemy, Emerald. They were laughing and smiling at each other like they were the best of friends. *When in the hell did that happen?* I thought to myself. I slowed down my running pace so I could watch them. It didn't take long for them to disappear into the hall that led to the juice bar. Well, that explains why his ring was missing.

A million assumptions began running through my head. None of them should have been there, but they appeared. Since when did those two become buddy-buddy? She can't even stand Myron; probably one of the reasons she tried to push him on me so hard. Suddenly, they're best friends? What the fuck ever. I don't have time for this nonsense. It was time for me to get out of here. I even lost my desire to do my run. After putting my clothes on I quickly ran for the front door. What I saw at the front desk was even more disturbing.

This bitch went from Myron to one of the trainers that work at the gym. I forget his name: Chance, Chase, Chauncey, something like that. Anyway, his name is irrelevant - much like she is - but it still makes me wonder. Is she screwing everyone with a penis up in here? I wouldn't be surprised if she was licking a few kitty cats, too.

She's so trifling; just watching her stand there and belittle herself was sickening. I guess losing me was the worst thing that's happened to her. She would never stoop down so low before. That clearly signals me ~~at~~ as the winner.

When she glanced my way her facial expression froze. I didn't linger long enough to see her reaction. I quickly turned my head and went out the door. I'm sure she was utterly embarrassed at her actions; I know I would have been. Then again, you would never catch me stooping to her level in any endeavor. When I walked past her car the urge to leave a few scratches hit me. I entertained the thought for a millisecond then decided against it. That's petty and beneath me; it's more like her hoodrat behavior. Instead, I pat the trunk of her car as if to signal my victory, laughed, then headed to my own vehicle. I can't wait until girl's night! This is going to make for some good entertainment

Emerald

Phoenix thinks she's slick. I know she saw me standing there talking to Chauncey. Poor girl just can't stand anyone besides her having a good time. Myron was right, she is starved for attention. Well I'm done feeding her sadistic ego. She was right; we should have ended our friendship a long time ago. If she only knew how much dirt I had on her I'm sure she would change her tune quick. It's okay though; as always I will have the last laugh.

"You okay, sweetheart?" Chauncey asked. He must have caught me zoning out.

"Yeah, boo, I'm fine."

"Then why are you staring off into space?"

"No reason." I responded. "No reason at all."

Earlier when I was talking to Myron at the juice bar he began questioning me about Phoenix and why she was trying so hard to get his attention. I figured that would happen. That girl has a sixth sense that goes off when she's being rejected. I don't see why it mattered. She didn't want him in the first place. He's currently separated so that's no longer an issue.

It's funny because the night we were together he went home and caught his wife in bed with another couple. Yes, I said couple; a homosexual couple on top of that. After beating the shit out of the two guys and throwing his wife out he came over to my house. Talk about being caught off guard. I was unprepared for his visit, but I don't think that mattered to him at that point in time.

"How does that work?" I remember asking him that night. "Oh, I'm sorry. That was insensitive of me."

"Don't worry about it. I'm trying to figure out the answer to that my damn self." He responded.

He continued to go on a tirade of derogatory names, words, and unsettling feelings. It got to the point where the only way I could shut him up was to distract him. Out came the alcohol and an hour later off came the clothes. I don't know what it is with men and their egos, but he had to remind himself that he loved women and used me as validation.

Honestly, he was a lot rougher compared to how he was in the shower. It felt good for a moment, and then it started to hurt. He kept mumbling to himself all sorts of comments; seemingly trying to reclaim his manhood. I don't see how it was in question though. It was his wife who was caught with two gay men; not him. At least that's the story I got. God only knows what really happened behind those doors. During his moment of climax he came so hard the condom almost slid off.

When I came back from cleaning up I could see tears in his eyes. He did his best to hide them - he wasn't going to let them fall in front of me; and to help keep him together I didn't say anything. I just handed him another shot of vodka and sat next to him. He grabbed my hand; I could feel his energy seep into me.

"Thanks."

"You're welcome."

That's all we said for the next three hours.
Ever since that night we've been a lot closer. He refuses to even utter his wife's name. As far as the men, there's been no mention of them either. It's probably better that way seeing as he was borderline ready to commit homicide. I indirectly offered myself to be his support system. Any time he needed someone to talk to, someone to hang with, or someone to verify his manliness I was there. We're kind of attached now. That wasn't part of my plan initially. I just wanted to disrupt the vibe between him and Phoenix. I got a little more than I bargained for, but knowing she's affected by his lack of attention made everything work out perfectly.

I should send her a tape.

The thought popped up in my head as I was driving home from the gym. That would really send her through the roof. Once she catches wind of how well-endowed he is and how much I can please him - and not her - she would be on fire! Hell, he can even send it to his wife. Why in the fuck do I care?! Revenge is the name of the game and we're ahead, bitches!

I thought about asking him about the idea. He'd probably go for it, but then it wouldn't seem authentic when we begin fucking the hell out of each other. It would be better to record it first and then bring the idea to him. There's nothing worse than a master plan ruined by expressing it before executing it. That's exactly what I'm going to do. The next time he calls or comes over distraught and horny the little red light will come on and the best sexual debauchery in the world will commence.

That opportunity came sooner rather than later.

"Hello?" I said, answering my phone half awake.

"Hey, I need to see you."

I turned over to look at the clock. It was almost four in the morning. *It's time.* That thought woke my ass up quick.

"I'll see you when you get here."

This was it; the moment I had been waiting for. Sure, I only had this idea a few hours ago, but I'm big on the power of intention and when I set something in motion shit just works out in my favor. I set my camera up in a location that wasn't obvious, placing the record button in an easy to reach area. Myron only lived about ten minutes away, but he never said where he was when he called. Keeping in mind that he could be as close as five minutes away I jumped in the shower and lathered up as quickly and efficiently as I could.

When I turned off the water I heard a knock at the door. I dashed to the room to turn on the camcorder. The dead space in the beginning can be edited out later. I pinned up my curls, sprayed on my favorite perfume that has yet to not drive a man wild, and answered the door.

"Now this is how a man should be greeted when he comes home."

His speech was slurred and his breath reeked of liquor. Yep, he was drunk, which means this footage was about to be golden. All I need is for him to make the first move and everything else will take care of itself.

I pulled him into the bedroom and turned on the red light. Just as I intended, he slowly slipped off my robe and laid me back on the bed. Now this was new because usually it's me that's going down on him. *Bonus points!* For fifteen minutes he dined on me, giving me the best head I've ever had in my life. Even Chauncey wasn't this good. That young buck could learn a thing or two from Myron.

When he stood up he was naked and fully exposed. I have no clue how he got his clothes off without me noticing nor did I care. I gave him a couple of quick strokes with my lips before he yanked my head back, pushed me down, and dove right into me. He took complete control over my body. We were skin to skin, intertwined with nothing in between us - not even a condom. That was a dumb move on my part, but I'm sure the sacrifice would be well worth the look on Phoenix and his wife's faces when they see just how much of a connection we shared.

Truth be told, this method was becoming a painful headache. Yeah, it was exciting in the beginning, but this went from me using Myron to him using me. That meant I was no longer in control. There's no vengeance if I'm not the one calling the shots. I'll give him this one because it's recording - and I'm going to work the hell out of the camera - but after tonight it's time to move on to something else. This is Laila's thing, not mine.

We were in the heat of the moment. I could tell he was almost ready to cum. As he sat on the edge of the bed I wrapped my legs around his waist and began riding the hell out of his dick. Facing the camera, I made as many exotic faces as I could; simulating the best love making session possible. I could feel his penis pulsating inside of me. He was about to burst. I began squeezing my vagina and rocking my hips in a figure-eight. Whenever I did this, he always moaned my name. This time he flat out screamed it. As he came inside of me I dug my fingers in his back and let out a soft moan. Just as he was finishing I slowly opened my eyes and flicked the camera off. Then we both collapsed on the bed.

"Damn it, you're the best!"

And that would signify the end of our session - and this part of revenge.

Laila

Everything was in order for girl's night. I had scheduled a private pole dancing class for us to attend. Afterwards, there was a male review a few blocks down the street. The theme of the night was *Hidden desires after dark!* I know I'm not the only damn freak in the group. Word on the street is that I may have some internal competition. Whatever; the street's word isn't always what it's cracked up to be.

Tomorrow night we'll see just who has an inner dominatrix waiting to come out. My money is on Summer. It's always the quiet ones you need to look out for. Either her or Emerald, my supposed competition. She's been doing a lot lately; almost to the point where she's beginning to scare the hell out of me. I think this breakup with Phoenix has gotten the best of her. The same can be said about Phoenix. They're like polar opposites of each other. One cares too much to the point of self-sabotage. The other one shuts down and doesn't give a damn at all. Neither method is healthy in my eyes. How they deal with their issues is on them. All I ask is peace on the home front. If either one of them mess up this night I will personally mess up their face.

I called Wren to verify that everything was ready for tomorrow. She didn't answer, but I was certain that she was home. Since I was only a few blocks away I decided to stop by her house. Her car was in the driveway. I hopped out the vehicle and went to knock on the door. The wind was cutting through the fabric of my maxi dress. My nipples started to pierce through, and I left my jacket in the car. Just as I turned to walk away the door opened.

"Girl what the…" I stopped myself soon as I saw Jason.
"Hey!" He said. "What's up?"
"Oh, hey Jase. Is Wren here?"
"No, she ran to the store real quick. Want to come in and wait for her?"

"Okay."

I walked in the house and he shut the door. We started engaging in small talk which wasn't out of the ordinary. Jason is such a cornball sometimes.

"What's going on with the ladies tomorrow?"

"Now you know if I told you Wren would kill me!" I said laughing.

We both sat on the couch. He was trying his hardest to get some information out of me, but I wasn't budging. And then he slightly began to cross the line. He wrapped his arms around me and began tickling me. He knows I'm freakishly ticklish. What he doesn't know is that's one of my major turn-ons. Without even thinking about who I was with I slipped my hand up his leg and grabbed him. In the blink of an eye we went from playing around as friends to making out as fornicators. It only lasted for a few seconds before we heard the screen door open on the other side.

When Wren opened the door we both snapped back to reality, playing it off as if we were just sitting there talking and laughing. I don't think Wren noticed anything as she had her hands full. Jason jumped up and went outside to grab the rest of the bags.

"Hey girl!" I said, trying to control my voice from shaking. "I tried to call you."

"Yeah, I saw. My bad. I couldn't answer because I was caught up with some non-English speaking cashier." Wren laughed sarcastically.

"Before you start, stop!" I warned her.

"But…never mind. What's up?"

"I wanted to fill you in on the goodness that is girl's night!"

"Spill it!"

I proceeded to tell her about what I had planned for us. She was getting more and more excited with each detail I released. This was a long time coming for her; hell, for all of us. Tomorrow was going to be a night of epic proportions.

"What about Phoenix and Emerald?" She asked me. "Did you hear anything from them?"

"Not since I spoke with them last time. Phoenix said she was coming, and Emerald said she wasn't. Maybe since it's been a few days she's changed her mind."

"I doubt it. You know they're both two sides of the same coin. Whatever they say is what they'll do. Oh well, I'm over it. Let's get this party started!"

"I'm with you, girl!"

"Oh shit, I forgot I have an appointment in an hour. Let me go get ready."

"Alright, Wren. I'll call you tonight."

"Okay, girl. Can you tell Jason to lock the door on your way out? He always forgets."

"I sure will."

Wren went upstairs to jump in the shower. Clearly, she was in a rush because I heard the water running before I grabbed my things to go. I walked out the door and came face to face with Jason. We looked at each other, wanting to finish what we started, but knowing we couldn't - well shouldn't - finish it.

"Listen…" he said.

I placed my finger to his lips.

"I won't tell if you won't."

He smiled, showing his bright white teeth. I never noticed it before, but he had a beautiful smile. I reached up to lightly kiss him on his cheek. His hand began to wrap around my waist. I pulled away so I wouldn't get caught up in the moment again. As I walked to my car, I could feel his eyes scanning my every move. It felt good and dirty at the same time. After all, this was my friend's man. They've been together for almost five years and not once have we come on to each other. I've known Wren since college; she trusts me. I can't break that bond. Not over a piece of dick, no matter how bad I wanted him.

When I got in my car, I saw him shut the door. I smiled and started up the engine. As I looked up, I could see the second story bedroom curtain move. At least I thought I did. Was she looking down on us the entire time? She couldn't have been because she was in the shower…I think. *Damn it!* I started to panic. Without delaying another second I pulled off, praying that she didn't see what just happened. If so, I had more than our friendship to lose. Wren is one person I pray to never cross in a bad way.

Wren

Jesus take the wheel.
Mohammed stand your ground.
Buddha keep the peace.
I'm about to fucking clown!

I said this mantra over and over as the scolding hot water caressed my body. There must have been a legitimate reason for what I saw happen downstairs. My eyes did not deceive me; she kissed his cheek. That's not what bothered me. Girls kiss guys on the cheek all the time. In fact, I've kissed plenty of her male hoes on the cheek. It's nothing. But the hand around the waist and that look in their eyes?

What the fuck was that about?

Let me chill out because I know I'm jumping to conclusions. Laila would never do that to me and Jason knows better. I laughed it off and got out the shower. Sometimes my imagination can get the best of me. The last thing I need on my mind is accusations of my man creeping with one of my best friends. That will never happen - not in a million years. They both respect me too much to do something like that. Well, Laila does anyway. Jason is just scared shitless to be that grimy with someone so close to me.

For the next few hours I went to my appointment and ran some errands. It took a few minutes, but I was finally able to shake that image out of my head. When I returned home Jason had cooked dinner for us. He had skills in the kitchen, so I was looking forward to what he prepared for us.

"It smells good in here." I said, placing my bags on the couch. "What's the special occasion?"

"Nothing special around here except for you! I got to make sure my place is on lock before y'all go man hunting tomorrow!" He smiled.

"Boy stop! You now I'm not going out to look for anyone else."

"I just want to be sure of that." He pulled me close to him. "You know I couldn't bear the thought of losing you."

"Who said you had to?"

He kissed the tip of my nose. I love when he does that. It makes me feel so good. I must admit he always knows how to smooth things over and make me smile.

"Go upstairs and wash up."

"Yes sir!"

I turned to go up the stairs as he smacked my ass. He was such a freak and I loved him for it. We had a nice dinner followed by some cuddling time in front of the television. A few shows and a few shots later we were sliding up and down each other's bodies in the living room. There's nothing like love making after a good meal and a good laugh. Thank goodness for this plush rug or we'd have a serious case of rug burn all over our bodies.

I woke up a couple of hours later to a loud ass infomercial, a cold, wet floor, and a cramp in my side. When I looked over at Jason he was sound asleep. As he lay there looking so peaceful, I couldn't help but to feel bad for all the times I fucked him over. He's never been directly caught with another woman, but I still let my anger get the best of me. Maybe it was time to let these feelings of insecurity go. Maybe it was just my ego getting in the way of what otherwise is a healthy, happy, functioning relationship.

My mind began to wander back to the day we met. He was so shy, sweet and sincere. I used to tease him all the time and tell him that chivalry should be his middle name. The way he treated me was new; most of the guys I had dated up to that point were the hit it and quit it type. Not him; he told me from the beginning he was looking for more and wanted to take his time to make sure we were a good fit. That was five years ago. He figured it out long before I did; we were indeed a good fit. It was high time that I got up to his level. I leaned over to kiss him on his forehead.

"Babe." I said softly. "Wake up, let's go to bed."
I tried to gently pull his arm.
"Stop, Laila." He mumbled.

My eyes felt like they were on fire. Did this mother fucker just call me Laila? I was literally two seconds away from boiling some grits to pour all over his ass. Now it all made sense: the dinner, the compliments, and the extra foreplay. He's hiding the fact that either he's fucked Laila, or he wants to fuck her. Either way it's unacceptable. I knew I wasn't imagining shit. He really has a thing for her. Makes me wonder how she feels about him. It's all good. I'll keep my cool until tomorrow night. Once she gets good and drunk, I'll find out all I need to know. That bitch can't keep shit tight when she's drunk; from her lips to her legs. I got up and walked into the bedroom, slamming the door behind me.

Let the mother fucking games begin!

Giuseppina

Gainell has been watching over me like a hawk since that outburst with Mr. Sandoval. I know she's concerned about me having a binge eating relapse, but I'm fine. It's becoming really aggravating having to explain every bite of food to her. I've gotten to the point where I don't even want to eat in front of her. Then she accuses me of starving myself. I'm not sure if she's aware of this or not, but her presence is only making this imaginary relapse idea of hers worse. I can't even have a celery stick without her giving me the stink eye. Thank goodness we'll be around all the girls tonight. I'll have a chance to breathe and eat a real meal.

This would be our last night out with everyone before we head off to take our mother to Italy. After this episode I wasn't looking forward to the trip anymore. Granted, my mother doesn't say as much as Gainell does about my eating habits, but she does get concerned. It's because she feeds off my sister's exaggerations; she's so damn convincing at times. The sad part about it is she's up for one hell of a challenge because we're going to Italy. I'm an Italian woman, and if there's one thing us Italian women can do it's eat. I will play the role of having control now because when I get my lips wrapped around some authentic Italian food you won't be able to stop me. And I feel sorry for the person that thinks otherwise.

"Nelli, shouldn't you go home to get ready for tonight?" I asked, hoping she would leave.

"I know what you're doing, GiGi, and it's not going to work. I already have my clothes in the car."

"You know what, this is ridiculous! I'm a grown ass woman, Nelli. I'm not going to eat myself into a coma."

"I don't think you understand how serious your problem is, GiGi."

"Oh really?" Now I was heated. "Well fine, Dr. Moreau. Why don't you explain it to me!"

"GiGi, you know it's not like that."

"I'm waiting."

She sat down next to me and placed her hand on top of mine. Here it goes: *I'm just worried about you*. Off she rattled with health statistics, my past reputation, and how I deal with anger. I admit that some of what she said was true, but that was no reason for her to medically diagnose me as too incompetent to handle my own dietary intake. Damn it, I'm half Italian. Carbs, sugars and starches are my friend. Hell, they're my birthright as well as hers. Just because she gets her rocks off in a different fashion doesn't make her any better or worse off than me.

"Okay, Nelli, I hear what you're saying. But has it ever occurred to you that I may feel the same way about you and your bad habit?"

"What bad habit?" She snapped back. "I don't have any bad habits."

"The hell you don't! You and I both know you would sell your soul if it would guarantee your every financial whim would be met."

"That's some bullshit, GiGi, and you know it."

"Do I? Then why do you try so hard to outdo me when it comes to business?"

"What the fuck are you talking about? I've always supported you and I don't appreciate you accusing me of doing otherwise!"

"Shut up and listen, damn! I know you support me, and I love you for that. But why is it whenever I land a major client or get a big bonus you damn near break your back to get someone or something bigger? Why can't you just be happy for me in that moment and not worry about how you can top me?"

"That's not fair, GiGi! I don't always do that."

"Oh, you don't? Should we check our phone records because it never fails that within forty-eight hours of me landing a client or receiving a bonus you contact me with some big break of your own."

"You're jealous that I outrank you?"

"Okay, let's get something straight right now. There is no jealousy here, sweetie!" I waved my finger in her face; she's officially made me mad. "What I'm saying is that you can't just sit with me in my happiness without trying to top it off with your own financial gain. I mean, damn, can I have a bigger slice of cake for once?"

"See, Gigi? You can't even make a point without relating it to food."

"Bitch, please! Everyone refers to money as cake! Don't act like it's just me!"

I took a deep breath. I don't like calling my sister out of her name. That is not in my character and she knows it.

"I'm sorry, Nelli. Listen, this isn't going how I want it to, and we need to start getting ready. Look, I love you for looking out for me, but some things you have to let me handle on my own, okay?"

"I now, GiGi, but sometimes you scare the shit out of me. The last time you binged you almost choked and died. If I hadn't walked in on you when I did…I can't have that on my conscience knowing I could have saved you."

"But you did save me, and I'm grateful to you for that. I can't promise I won't turn to food for comfort, but I can promise that if it gets to the point where it's the only thing that comforts me then I'll reach out to you. Deal?"

I extended my hand to her. She stared at it for a minute.

"I can't promise you a deal, but I will back off a little bit. I'm your big sister. It's my job to look out for you."

"Two minutes does not give you big sister status."

"The hell it doesn't!"

We grabbed each other and hugged. If there's one thing I love about Nelli it's that no matter how many of her buttons I push she's always there for me. I could probably burn her entire house down, spend all her money, and sell all her possessions and she'd still be on my side. She would kill anyone else, but we have a special bond; one that I thank God for every day.

"Come on, girl." I said. "Let's go get sexified and show these bitches how it's really done!"

"Damn skippy! And here." Gainell said, handing my candy bar to me. "You deserve this. Just don't let it go to your head."

"Fuck my head! This can make a beeline to the bust line, for real! Get my little B's buzzing!"

"You are a mess!" Gainell laughed at me.

"At least I'm a sexy one!"

We headed upstairs to get ready for tonight. I must admit, it felt good to know my sister really did care about me. That's something I'm very grateful for and will never take for granted. She doesn't have to concern herself with my life, but if she sees that I'm in trouble she will intervene. She probably did save my life when she stepped in before. I would never tell her that, though. Admitting that I have a weakness is a weakness of mine. Maybe it's a good thing she can see what I have trouble acknowledging.

In a couple of hours we were finally ready for our night of debauchery. We took a couple of pre-party shots at my place before heading off to meet Wren and the girls. Normally, we'd all go out for girl's night together. This time we're meeting at the location for whatever reason. I'm anxious to see if Emerald will show up. I know Phoenix will be there; her ego will not let her back down even if she knows she's dead wrong. Emerald, on the other hand, is a bit timid and might fly off the handle if we show more attention to Phoenix than to her. This is going to be interesting.

Summer

I have been waiting for this night all week long. Now I don't feel like going. This always happens to me when something exciting is going on. I get all amped up and ready to roll and when it comes time I hide in my shell. This cycle must end; it's getting me nowhere. My bed was so comfortable and inviting. There was no reason why I should abandon it for a night full of mystery and uncertainty.

Yet the girls were expecting me to come. They've been calling me every day to make sure I show up. Wren even said she'll kidnap me if I'm not there. I guess I have no choice but to go. I tried to convince myself this would be good for me. Besides work I'm always stuck in this damn house. That can drive a person insane. I know because I was staring insanity in the face.

Might as well get up and get it over with.

It took every ounce of energy that I had to get out of bed. Once I got the music going and took a few shots I started to feel better. By the time I got finished getting dressed, my mood was ten times better. Now all I had to do was hurry up and get to the girls before I lost my spark.

I went for my keys when my cell phone rang. It was Laila. They were hunting me down already.

"Hey girl!" I said. "I'm on my way out the door."

"Wait, before you leave, I need to talk to you."

From the sound of her voice I was about to lose my buzz real fast.

"Is it bad?" I asked while going for my bottle.

"Yes, so sit down, shut up, and let me finish the story before you say a word."

"Laila, what did you do?"

"I kissed Jason."

The bottle slipped out of my hand. Thank goodness it was a thick bottle, or it surely would have shattered. I know this girl did not just tell me she kissed Wren's fiancé. Her life was going too well for her to have a death wish.

"What the fuck is wrong with you, Laila?" I blurted out. "Are you ready to die or something?"

"I know, I know! That's why I called you. I feel so bad. It was an accident; it just happened!"

"How did it just happen?"

She proceeded to tell me how the entire scenario played out. In a way, I can see how she would think it was innocent, but she also crossed the line. She had just as much power to stop it as he did, but she didn't. Then she tells me about her leaving and how he grabbed her. The kiss on the cheek just exacerbated the situation. When she said she thinks Wren saw them she really freaked out.

"Oh my God, Wren is going to curse you out!"

"No, that's the innocent part. It gets worse."

"How in the hell can it get any worse than that?" I knew I would regret asking that question, but I had to know.

"When she left for her appointment, he called me."

"And…"

"He asked me to meet him somewhere."

"So, did you?"

"Yes, but we only had one drink."

"Well, that's innocent enough I guess."

"Wait, there's more."

"Damn it, Laila!"

"We went back to their house. I told him how I felt about what happened earlier and how we can't do that to Wren."

"That's good."

"He agreed. So we kissed, had sex, made up, and that was that."

"You. Did. WHAT?!"

Thus began the argument of all arguments between me and Laila. She's done a lot of grimy things in the past, but this one took the cake. If there is one line you never cross it's the line between your friend and her man. In a few minutes she managed to destroy a perfectly loving relationship, a strong friendship, and her entire life. I'm laid back about a lot of things, but friendship, loyalty, and trust are not on that list.

"You have to tell her." I said sternly.

"Bitch are you off your rocker? I can't tell Wren that I fucked her man! That's why I called you!"

"Well I'm not telling her and she needs to know, Laila. You owe her that. Who would you rather she hear it from: him or you?"

"Neither one, and she's not going to find out! Got it?"

"Oh no, baby girl, we're not going there! You will not bully me into keeping your dirty secret. It's not my place to tell, but at the same time she's going to find out. Have you forgotten who you're dealing with? This is Wren we're talking about here. When she gets angry the devil gets nervous!"

"I know that, Summer! Even more reason she can never find out. Look, we vowed to never let it happen again. I don't even have a desire to go there with him again. Hell, I had to go fuck someone else immediately after to get rid of the guilt."

"That doesn't make the situation any better and it doesn't erase what you've already done."

"Listen to me, please! I called you for comfort, not criticism. I know what we did was wrong. I know I betrayed Wren's trust and I fell into Jason's trap. Okay, maybe he didn't trap me, but none of that matters right now. All I care about is getting this off my chest so I can forget about it and move on with my life. That's it. Can you come open the door?"

"What?"

I heard her knocking at the front. When I opened the door she was standing in front of me with tears flooding from her eyes. The poor child looked like she just lost her best friend. If word gets out about what she did she had more than that to lose. My anger and frustration towards her quickly turned into sympathy.

"Is it that obvious?" She asked, regarding the expression on my face.

"Yeah, it is."

I stepped to the side for her to come in. Laila walked past me sulking like a little girl who just got her bike stolen. I closed the door behind us and went to sit next to her on the couch. There wasn't much I could say to make her feel better. She knew she was in a whirlwind of trouble, but tonight was not the night for anything to come out. Somehow, some way, we had to come up with a plan to keep this swept under the rug for at least tonight. After that, she's on her own.

"What were you thinking, Laila?" I came right out and asked. "Did it not cross your mind that out of the thousands of men in the city to not pick Jason?"

She slid into the couch and sulked louder. Right now was not the best time to run a guilt trip on her. What she needed was a good, stiff drink. It was starting to look like I would be driving tonight. Thank goodness she's the type to get silent when she gets drunk or else it would be over for her.

Cognac and coke were the first thing I could think of to take her edge off. I started to mix her a drink. When I turned around to get the soda out of the fridge, she was taking the bottle of Hennessey to the head. She was clearly stressed and on edge. I can't say that I could relate to her pain, but I could relate to her fear. Not knowing the outcome of something has got to be the most feared plague of mankind.

"Laila, put that down!" I commanded her. "What good is drinking the entire bottle going to do?"

"Weren't you about to make me a drink anyway?"

"Yes, a drink. One drink. Not one gallon! Get over here!"

I dragged her from the kitchen back to the living room. She would not let the bottle go. This was a moment to pick and choose my battles and right now the bottle was winning. My strength was being reserved for later tonight just in case I needed it.

"Listen to me, Laila. I'm your friend and I'm on your side, you know that. I'm also Wren's friend and stand by her just as much. What I'm suggesting you do is going to hurt - physically and emotionally - but she deserves to know. It's her right to decide if she wants the relationship with either you or Jason to continue. You're so focused on covering your ass, have you even stopped to think about her? What if this isn't the first time he's stepped out on her? What if he's already told her and made it seem like you came onto him? This is already an ugly situation, but if you don't take control of it this very second it's only going to get worse."

I couldn't tell if she was listening to me or not, but I had to keep trying to get through to her. We already had enough friction within the group between Phoenix and Emerald. If they both decide to show up tonight that would be another center stage event we would have to deal with. Then there's Gainell and Giuseppina. Those two are always a handful with their hot-headed Italian asses. Shit, from the looks of it I might be the only sane one in the group. See, it pays to be low key and under the radar.

It took a while, but Laila finally was able to look me in the eyes.

"You're right, Summer. You're absolutely right about everything. Wren deserves to know, and she should hear it from me."

"I'm glad you feel that way."

"But she's been looking forward to this night for weeks. I've already pretty much destroyed her life and trust in me. Can I at least give her this one night and talk to her tomorrow? There's going to be enough tension in the air. This will only add fuel to the fire. Plus, I need to mentally prepare myself for this. After all, it will probably be the last conversation I'll ever have with her."

Laila collapsed in my lap and began to cry. She wasn't as hysterical now; that was when she was in full panic mode. Now it was more of a mournful expression. The death of their friendship was at her door and she knew she would have to answer it sooner rather than later. I just pray she can do it on her own terms and that Wren hasn't caught wind of what happened yet.

We sat for an hour or so before we decided to go. It wasn't unlike us to be late to these events anyway; we always showed up together or a few minutes apart from each other.

"Are you ready?" I asked, before heading to the door.

"As ready as I'll ever be." She said while refreshing her makeup. "Listen, Summer, thanks for being there for me. I hope this doesn't affect our friendship as well."

"Not at all. You're a human and you made a mistake. Even Wren will have to admit to that. No matter what happens between you two I will always be there for you."

"Thanks, girl. I love you!"

She embraced me with a passionate hug, as if she didn't want to let me go.

"I love you, too. Now let's get out of here. Remember, tonight is about fun! We'll face reality tomorrow."

"Yes, ma'am!"

We both let out a good laugh. After tossing back one more shot of cognac and coke we were ready to hit the town.

Emerald

"Damn it, Emma, you are one sexy bitch!"

I laughed as I stared at myself in the mirror. This fiery red dress accentuated all my deep curves. Adding to it my long, red ringlets and I was one red robin hood ready to take on the biggest and baddest of wolves. Tonight was the night I would unleash my master plan against Phoenix. The tape was only part of the show. What would happen to her afterwards is something that only an act of God could prevent. Just thinking about her life crumbling right before her eyes brought a smile to my face. Vindictive? Yes, but also very necessary.

This has been a long time coming and I was set to enjoy every second of it. I had some time to kill so I gave Chauncey a call. He asked if he could stop by since he was in the area. I knew what he wanted, but there was no way I could duplicate this look. As much as I would love to ride the hell out of his dick right now, I had to take a rain check.

I called all my people to make sure everything was in place. It was a good thing Laila gave me a play by play of what we were doing tonight. Each stop was sure to piss her off more than the last. When we end things at the pole dancing class that's when I'll strike with the video. What's even funnier is that Myron's wife is supposed to be in the building as well. I can't name one chick that won't give into the temptation of overhearing an argument. Once she hears her name and the sound of her man giving me the business, I'm sure she'll come trolling over. He can thank me for that later.

But even with the video being present that's still not the grand finale. Not to give away any spoilers, but I do hope she has a good therapist on standby. She's going to need it to overcome her past…again. Half of the things that's about to conspire she probably thinks I've long forgotten. And some of them I have, but thanks to some research and great journal keeping skills of the past I have enough dirt to grow a garden of her sins.

For years Phoenix has been so full of herself; standing on some imaginary pedestal that she feels is her birthright. Too many times she has looked down on me and others just like me. Sure, she has it good, but there are millions out there who have it way better. She knows this, but she would never admit it. Her tricks and antics to get what she wants have been outrageous, and in some cases, illegal. Being prideful can ruin your life. She'll understand this once and for all in just a few short hours.

Just before it was time to leave, I ran through my plan one more time. There would be four series of events that were strategically created to break her down. The first would be seeing her ex-fiancé, Jordan, and his new wife. He dumped Phoenix for this woman, and she was hot and heartbroken at the same time. Jordan has no idea he's going to see Phoenix tonight, but he also has no unresolved feelings about their defunct relationship. This encounter will be interesting.

After hitting her emotionally, the next step is to burn her socially. This will be done at the night club where a surprise song dedication and message will be played in front of everyone. Not only does she hate to be publicly humiliated, she despises the song because it was attached to a bad memory. A few years ago, Phoenix and I went to an event and were rear ended by a couple of guys. They were blasting this song from their car. When Phoenix got out to check the damage and confront them, both guys jumped in the car and sped off. They never did catch them, and the repairs cost her almost two thousand dollars to fix.

Next would be a slight physical altercation. This one will be tricky because the person must strike when none of us are around. I know these girls and they will kick off the shoes and slap on the Vaseline in a heartbeat to protect each other. The assailant I hired doesn't know Phoenix personally, but it's not difficult to find someone willing to slap the shit out of another person for $100. A crack head would have done it for less, but I wanted to choose someone that would not stand out.

I'm sure it'll take about a good hour or so after that incident before we head off to our pole dancing party. That's when the last and final attack would strike. I've been to Lollipop Land before and they typically show a video of the pole dancing techniques. Their video has been replaced with a mash-up of a few sex scenes that some of her past lovers have oh so graciously provided to me. Then it wraps up with my own performance getting it on with her newfound crush that she just can't have. If that doesn't send her world crashing around her then I don't know what will.

Will the girls get mad at me? Probably. But I'm not worried about that. Vengeance requires sacrifice and I'm willing to put my friendships with them on the line just to make Phoenix suffer. Besides, they're probably all on her side anyway. No one ever goes to bat for me. Whatever happens they'd better be careful; they could easily be my next target.

"Well, Emma, it's now or never. Time to ruin that bitch's life for good."

With one more look in the mirror I stepped out of the house and got in my car. The next time I enter my threshold will be after sweet, sweet victory has been claimed in my honor. This would be a long night. I plan on making every second worth it.

Phoenix

For the past few hours I've had this ill feeling in my stomach. Something was going to happen tonight, but I don't know what it could be. Everyone seems to be on one accord with girl's night - at least as far as I know. What in the hell is going on with me? Whatever it is I need to be on alert just in case something happens. It was hard to get my mind off this feeling. I had to figure it out.

I went into the spare bedroom and turned off all the lights. After lighting a candle, I sat in silence until whatever it is that I needed to know came to me. Some might call this process meditation. I'm not big on all of that. All I know is whenever I feel like this something is about to go down and I need to be on my guard big time. As I sat there, I thought of everyone that I knew of to see if the feeling got stronger, weaker, or stayed the same. Through family, co-workers, and friends it never fluctuated. Then I started to think about my girls. Suddenly, I felt violently ill.

There wasn't one person who set this feeling off. I just shifted my thoughts to tonight and could barely control my stomach. Whatever was about to happen had to do with the group. An internal battle brewed inside of me. I had to warn them, but what was I going to say? How would I say it and what would they think? There is no way I'm about to put myself on the line because of some ill feeling. The only thing I could do is stand guard and be prepared for whatever was about to be thrown our way.

When I finally left the room I was drained and emotional. Part of me didn't even want to go out anymore, but I couldn't leave the girls to fend for their own lives. I had to be there and act as a guard against…what? I still didn't know, but it was something. My internal alarm would be on high alert throughout the entire night. It wouldn't stop me from having fun, but I would be on high alert.

I went back to getting ready. My mood had completely shifted. What started off as extreme excitement has now turned into complete caution and concern for my friends. Maybe it had to do with that extra chick that might show up. I wasn't sure, but for her sake I hope not. She's not on the protection list. She can and will catch an ass whooping if I even remotely begin to suspect her.

Alright, girl, let's refocus.

It was time to shift gears. I turned on some hip-hop music, tossed back a couple of shots, and officially had my own pre-party. A few shots later I was feeling myself and ready for whatever the night had to bring. Before stepping out I made sure I packed my fully charged taser, switch blade, mace, and brass rings. I dare someone to fuck with me tonight. Feeling safe and satisfied I was ready to hit the ground running. Let's make this a night to remember.

Wren

So many thoughts were running through my head as I made my way to Villa Aurora where we were meeting for dinner. Ever since last night I haven't been myself. Why in the hell would Jason say Laila's name unless there was something going on between them? It made perfect sense and no sense at the same time. As much as I tried to fight the reality that maybe they were creeping, the evidence kept stacking against me. He wasn't always underneath me so there was no telling what he was doing when I wasn't around. Monogamy is not his strong point. I understand that and accepted it because I always had a way to pay him back. This is a little different though. Now there were two people who would feel my wrath if my assumptions are true. One way or another I was going to find out tonight.

I sat in the parking lot for a while thinking about how I was going to handle the situation. If anything was going to be said it had to be done quickly. Once Laila's drunk, she becomes as silent as a mouse. Then there was absolutely zero chance of me finding anything out. I had a small window of opportunity, usually between her third and fifth drink, before she shuts down. Whatever I planned to do had to be executed fast. Just as I was contemplating my approach, I saw Laila and Summer pull into the parking lot. I looked over in the car, smiled and wave. Laila looked like she had panic written all over her face. I'm sure Summer gave her a couple of shots to calm her down from whatever she was feeling. That just made me even angrier because if Summer knows something and doesn't tell me she will catch hell, too. No assumption will be made yet; let's just see how this night goes.

Calm down. Take a deep breath. You can do this, Wren. Keep your cool.

"Hey ladies!" I said as perky as possible while stepping out of the car.

"Hey girl!" They said in unison.

We all gave each other a hug. When I hugged Laila I noticed her heart was racing.

"What's wrong girl?" I asked her. "Is everything okay?"

She shot a quick look to Summer who looked past her.

"Yeah, everything's fine. I just had an off day, that's all. I'm so ready for tonight!"

"You and me both!" Summer said, trying to interject.

"Well then, let's get started. Everyone else should be on their way. Let's go get our table."

We walked into the restaurant and were led to our table. The evening started off with light talk. I didn't probe Laila too much about her "off day" for the simple fact that I knew that wasn't the real problem. So long as I got my info confirmed within that window I would have all the evidence that I needed to confront her. I'm not looking for a confession; just a slip of the lips would suffice.

Gainell and Giuseppina walked in about ten minutes after we did. We all gave each other a hug. The waiter came around to take their drink order. As Gainell was finishing her order we saw Phoenix walk up to the table.

"Well hello, beautiful ones!" Phoenix said excitedly.

"Phoe!" We all yelled in unison.

The energy of the group was mixed, but we did our best to mask it by being positive and happy. On the surface we all looked like we were riding on cloud nine. Underneath it all, I had a feeling we all were facing some major obstacles - individually and with each other.

After another round of hugs and another round of drink orders we began to look over the menu. It seemed as if everyone who was going to show up was here. Our guard was down and we started to relax a little bit. Then out the corner of my eye I saw a woman walk up to us. She was in all red, from her hair to her shoes, and her figure was on point. I looked up and almost dropped my menu.

"Emma? Is that you?!"

All the girls, Phoenix included, looked up in astonishment. It's been about a month since any of us have seen Emerald, and I had to admit she looked amazing. There was not a trace of sorrow or sadness on her. That usually spelled trouble for someone else. Please, God, don't let that happen tonight.

"Girl you look sexy as hell!" Laila said.

"I love that dress!" Gainell followed up.

One after one we complimented her; well, everyone except for Phoenix. She sat and smiled as if she had something planned for tonight as well. I dismissed the thought in hopes that my ego was creating stories again.

"Thank you, ladies!" Emerald said. "I've been putting in some overtime at the gym. It's amazing what a few extra workouts can do for your body and self-esteem!"

She sat down, of all places, right next to Phoenix. The tension in the air became thick as steel. Everyone at that table was on edge - except for them.

"Hey, Phoenix. I haven't seen you in a while. How are you, hon?"

We couldn't tell if she was being condescending or genuine. Phoenix's reply would either make or break this entire night.

"You must be Emerald. It's nice to meet you."

Phoenix immediately reached for her glass and took a drink. *Here we go!* I thought to myself this was going to be a long night with these two. But surprisingly Emerald didn't take offense.

"You're so funny, Phoenix. You still got it!" Emerald quickly changed the subject. "So has anyone ordered their meal yet?"

"Not yet." Giuseppina said. "We're still deciding on what to get."

"Yay! I didn't miss anything!" Emerald began to browse the menu while talking. "I feel like I've been so out of the loop lately! Fill me in, ladies. What's been going on?"

One by one we began to update her on our lives. She was showing genuine interest without interjecting her own fears and insecurities. This was a different Emerald than the one we were used to hanging around. This Emerald had a certain aura about her that was strong and confident; not one that was always needy and dependent. I could get used to her being like this. After speaking with everyone else she asked me how things were going. This opportunity was about to work in my favor.

"How about you, Wren?" Emerald asked. "How are things going with you and Jason?"

The question of the night.

"Honestly, I don't know, Emma."

"What do you mean?" Gainell interjected. "What's going on?"

"Well, he's been acting funny for a while. That's nothing new. But last night when I tried to wake him up to go to bed, he slipped up and called me someone else's name."

The entire table went into a silent uproar. I could tell the ladies were pissed. When I looked at Laila, she was damn near choking on her drink. *Keep playing the role, Wren. It's working.*

"He did what?" Phoenix asked. "What name did he say?"

"I couldn't make it out. It sounded like Jada, Kayla, Shayla…I don't know. Whatever it was ended in an "a" and when I find out that's what I'm getting into - someone's A as in ass!"

"That's messed up," Summer said, "but do you think it's really worth it?"

"Yes, Summer, I do. He's been doing this to me for far too long. I thought we were over that phase, but I guess I was wrong. To me, an ass whooping is definitely in order." I paused, and then looked at her and Laila. "For him and for her."

I said it so calmly that it sent her into a panic. She excused herself and headed to the restroom. She was on her third drink and was ready to break. When she comes back that's when I'll get the rest of my information.

"Maybe I should go check on her." Summer said.

"Why?" Emerald asked the question before I could. She's working in my favor more than I expected. "Is something wrong with her?"

"No, she just had a similar issue and is feeling some kind of way."

"Oh, really?" I interjected.

"Yeah."

"What happened?" I asked.

"I don't know the details. I just know that she came by my house earlier all upset. I gave her a couple of shots to calm her down.

"Wait, so she's already been drinking?"

"Yeah, we both had a couple of shots. Come on, Wren! You know we all have a few shots before meeting up!" Summer tried to laugh it off, but I didn't think it was funny.

My drink count was off. She was on her fifth drink of the night already. If she had another one and sat for too long my window of opportunity was shot to hell. I had to think fast if this was going to work in my favor.

"Maybe I should go check on her." I said.

Before Summer could interject Laila came back to the table.

"Hey, girl, is everything okay?" Giuseppina asked.

"Yeah, I'm cool." Laila said.

"What happened?" I asked. "Summer said you were having a similar issue with one of your knuckleheads. Whose ass do I need to beat in addition to Jason's?"

Laila looked at Summer as if to have a telepathic conversation with her. Then she turned to me.

"It's not worth it."

She shrugged her shoulders as the waiter came up and brought her another drink.

"Here's the drink you ordered from the bar, ma'am." He said.

She smiled and grabbed her drink. That's where she went; she was at the bar not in the bathroom. My window was officially closed, but thanks to her protective action I had all the information that I needed. There was something going on between her and Jason. Little does she know Summer just confirmed it by trying to cover up for her. Her sneaking away to grab another drink so she wouldn't talk was the last nail in the coffin. Emerald was usually a pain in my ass, but tonight I appreciated her more than ever. Thanks to her questioning I now had an official pass to whoop someone's ass.

Gainell

Everyone seemed to be on edge tonight. This was supposed to be fun for all of us; a chance to let go of our everyday worries and just have fun. Whatever is going on with this group needs to seize and desist at once. I already had enough on my plate; there was no room left for added drama. Besides, I had to keep my eye on my sister. She was still quite vulnerable after her blow-up the other day. If she could maintain control during dinner everything else would be a piece of cake.

Wren kept asking Laila questions about what happened with her and whatever dude pissed her off this week. Laila, on the other hand, wasn't saying a word. I could tell it was irritating Wren, but I didn't understand why. This wasn't anything new and usually Wren would just drop the subject. But she kept making side comments comparing her situation to Laila's. Something was up between them two and it had to do with a man.

Oh hell no!

For the love of God, I hope Laila didn't stoop so low as to have slept with Wren's man. That would be an instant funeral for her and trial for Wren. It's a spoken understanding to never mess with anyone's man, past or present. I was certain Laila learned her lesson after Wren beat her ass in college.

After that scenario we haven't had to worry about Laila crossing the line again. It was one of the reasons she was so diligent about letting us know her current fling's name. It was a stat check with all of us to make sure he's in the clear. Based on the past there's no way that's the problem. I just wish I knew what it was.

The waiter finally came back around to take everyone's order. One by one we ordered our meals. My sister and I were last. I went before her so I could order for the both of us.

"Can we have two orders of shrimp linguini with a side of Caesar salad?"

"What type of dressing for your salad?"

"Light Italian for me and Light balsamic vinaigrette for my sister."

"Anything else?"

"Yes, I'll have a…"

My sister started to add to her order, but I stopped her.

"No, that'll be all. Thanks."

I grabbed her menu with mine and handed it to the waiter.

"What the fuck, Nelli!" Giuseppina snapped. "I'm not two years old. I can order my own damn food!"

"I'm doing you a favor, GiGi." I tried to reassure her. "Besides, this is what you said you wanted."

"That doesn't give you the right to order it for me. What if I changed my mind?"

"Whoa!" Phoenix interjected. "What's going on with you two?"

"Yeah, what's up?" Emerald asked. Phoenix seemed irritated that she followed up right behind her.

"Nelli thinks I'm binging again." Giuseppina said. "A client upset me the other day and I had a moment."

"What kind of moment?" Summer asked.

"I got so upset that I started eating a lot. It was no big deal. It only happened on that day in that moment. I haven't done it since."

"Yeah, because I've been there to stop you!" I said.

"Oh, shut the hell up, Nelli! I can control my eating habits and don't need you or anyone else to babysit me. You act like I took down an entire damn cow! It was a couple of candy bars and some chocolate milk! For Pete's sake calm the fuck down about it!"

"Ladies, you're getting loud." Wren said. "Tone it down a notch."

"Wren's right." I said. "Let's not do this here, Gigi. We're supposed to be out having fun, not arguing and bickering like little kids."

"Exactly, Nelli! We're not little kids. Not you…and certainly not me."

"Fine!" I said, and threw my hands up. "Eat your way to the grave, I don't care! Let these mother fuckers send you spiraling out of control in a bowl of spaghetti. *A torto si lagna del mare chi due volte ci vuol tornare.*"

"*Il tuo nemico è quell dell' are tua.*" Giuseppina replied.

"Fuck that! We need English, people!" Wren said, laughing.

Everyone laughed except for Giuseppina and me. To us this was far from being hilarious. We have been dealing with her eating problem since she was a child and the same thing always triggers it: someone upsets her and she doesn't know how to handle it.

"I said I'm done, GiGi, and I meant it. You don't have to worry anymore about me interfering again."

I excused myself from the table to go to the restroom. Giuseppina had upset me beyond words by her outburst. I wasn't out to bite or even spite her. I was trying to be a good sister and alert her to the error of her own ways. Maybe she didn't need me to look out after her. Sometimes, when you really love someone you have to let them fall on their face. As much as I hate to do it, I have no choice but to fall back on this one. Phoenix came in the restroom to check on me.

"Hey girl, are you okay?"

"Yeah, I'm fine. It just hurts, you know. I hate to see GiGi fall apart like that. What's worse is that she doesn't even see it herself."

"What happened to her?"

I proceeded to tell Phoenix what happened at Giuseppina's office the other day. No one else knew what was going on with her so our outburst seemed out of place. Once I filled her in she had a better understanding of the situation.

"Nelli, I love you girl, but you have to let Gigi fight her own battles."

"Do you think I was wrong for stepping in?" I said defensively.

"Absolutely not! If someone was disrespecting my sister like that all hell would break loose. What I'm saying is that your concern shouldn't have gone beyond that day. All you're doing is delaying her healing process which will only make her binging worse. She would have been over it by now if you weren't still focused on it."

"You think she would, but she keeps shifting the focus off herself and onto me."

"How is that?"

"Instead of talking about her binging problem she seems to think I have my own problem to focus on."

"What problem is that?"

"She thinks I'm money hungry."

"Well, shit, you are!"

At that moment there was nothing I could do but walk away. I heard her call out for me, but I was done with the entire situation. I left the restroom just as another woman was coming in. I could hear her talking to Phoenix as the door shut. It must be someone she knows.

Phoenix

"Hey, Phoenix. Long time no see."

I have no clue who this random woman is, but if she want's drama then I got it for her.

"Excuse me, but do I know you?"

"Not directly, but I believe you're the reason my man and I were having problems a few months ago. You know Jordan, right?"

"Oh, you're one of those women. Listen, I'm not sure who you're referring to, but I guarantee I'm not the cause or effect of anyone's failed relationship."

"Oh no, honey. No one said we failed. He's happy at home and thanks to you he finally realizes that."

She had this smirk on her face as if she was trying to get one over on me. She didn't know me as well as she thought. Otherwise, she'd realize it's impossible for me to give a fuck about any random dude…hers included.

"I'm sorry, sweetie, but clearly you don't know me as well as you think you do. I don't know a Jerry…"

"Jordan."

"Whoever it is, I don't know him, nor do I recognize the name so I can't be the one you're referring to."

"Sure you are. You stay on Austeria Lane, right? And you have a dark blue Mercedes convertible…used, right? I know more about you than you think I do."

Now this bitch was starting to piss me off. Who in the hell was she and how did she know all this stuff about me? That sick feeling I had in the pit of my stomach earlier came rushing back. This must be the reason why. My girls weren't far away so I wasn't worried about taking her down, but she really needed to be worried about me.

"Who in the hell do you think you are, bitch?" I snapped. "Do you have a death wish or something?"

She laughed in my face. That made me even angrier.

"No need for threats, honey. I just came in to say thank you for helping my man realize he had a real woman by his side all along. I guess your pussy wasn't as golden as you said it was."

She turned on her heels and walked away.

"Dirty trick!" She said as the door closed behind her.

My skin felt like it was on fire. I know his whore did not just try to throw shade at me! Mentally I wanted to go hunt her down and shock the shit out of her with my Taser. She could be personally introduced to every weapon that was currently in my bag. By the time I calmed down enough to move she was nowhere in sight. I lost all senses of what was going on before that moment. The last thing I needed to bring back to the table was another issue. Plus, I never let anyone see me rattled. Never! I splashed some water on my face and pulled myself together.

When I got back to the table I was reminded of the conversation Gainell and I just had in the bathroom. Surely she knew I was only playing with her to lighten the mood. I sat down between her and that other chick, reached over to grab her hand and gave it a squeeze. That was as close to an apology as anyone has ever received from me. She smiled and squeezed my hand back. We were cool again.

As I looked towards the door I saw the girl from the bathroom leaving with a guy. He did look familiar. In fact, I knew exactly who he was. It had been so long since we spoke that I must have blocked him out. My heart began to race thinking back to the things she was saying to me. When he looked back our eyes met for a brief second. He quickly turned around and walked out with her right behind him. In the last second, I caught her giving me the finger. Next think I know I'm running after her ass.

Laila

"Phoenix, no!" I yelled as we all went after her.

We all caught up with her outside; she was pacing back and forth like she was looking for someone. The look on her face signaled that she was ready to kill. I walked up and put my hands on her shoulders.

"What are you doing out here?"

"Where is she?" She shouted, looking past me. "Where is that bitch?"

"Who?" Summer asked.

She stopped in her tracks. Whoever this person is ticked her off big time, but she never said her name. She started pacing back and forth again as if to justify her reason for coming outside.

"Yeah, you better run, bitch! Don't nobody want your funky ass man anyway!"

After yelling at the top of her lungs for what seemed like forever she went back into the restaurant as if nothing ever happened. The rest of us stood outside looking around at each other.

"What was that all about?" Gainell asked. "She was fine a second ago."

"I don't know, but let's get back inside." Summer said.

"Yeah, let's go." I said.

I held the door open for everyone to go inside. Emerald was the last one to go in before me. I swore I saw a smirk on her face. As she walked by I grabbed her arm.

"Did you know something about this?" I asked.

"No, I didn't." She said and continued to go inside.

Something told me to keep my eye on her for the rest of the night. As if I didn't have my own mouth to watch, now I had to add her actions to the list? I let out a deep sigh and followed everyone back to the table. The restaurant patrons were all staring at us. We played it off as if we didn't see all eyes on us. Emerald sat down and that same smirk came across her face. Phoenix was in a world of her own, trying to hold it together.

"Alright y'all, let's get this party jumping again." Giuseppina said as she signaled for the waiter.

We all ordered another round of drinks and each had a shot of tequila. After ten minutes it was as if the fiasco outside never happened. Our meals arrived and we had a wonderful time. The food was great, the conversation was even better, and somehow everyone at the table was getting along. Even the issue between Gainell and Giuseppina calmed down. She ordered what she wanted and Gainell didn't say a word. Once we all ate our meals and paid our tabs, we left to go see a movie.

When I got in the car with Summer, I began to freak out again.

"She knows, Summer! I know she does."

"What makes you think that?"

"Did you not hear the questions she was asking me? That name she heard Jason say was my name! I know it was!"

"You don't know that, Laila. You're freaking out for nothing. Well, there's a reason, but you're reading more into it than is really there."

"What made her think something was wrong with me then? She's toying with me, Summer, and you know it. This is how she does before she strikes. I'm about to be her next victim."

Summer reached into the seat pocket behind me. She pulled out a mini shot glass filled with liquor. She carries them with her almost everywhere she goes.

"Here." Summer said, handing me the ready-made shot glass. "Drink this and calm down."

"What is this?" I said looking it over.

"Twisted Shots, girl! It's the same thing I always have with me, just a new flavor. This one is Orange with whipped vanilla. Trust me; you need this in your life right now."

I took the shot and tossed it back. It went down smooth and tasted good.

"Do you have another one."

She produced the remaining four pack and placed it in my lap.

"You need them more than I do right about now. Besides, I have more in the trunk."

"Summer, I'm worried about you." I said. "You drink an awful lot. Maybe you should slow down a bit."

"No, I'm good." She said. "I need something to keep me going. Otherwise, I'd just lay up in my apartment and do nothing."

"But this is a bit extreme, don't you think? I've never met anyone that has liquor stored in their trunk for ready access."

"You have. You just don't know they do it."

"If you say so."

I pulled the top off the next shot and took that back just as fast as the first one.

"Be careful with those things, Laila. They sneak up on you."

By the time she completed her sentence I was already on the last one. I placed the little cups in a bag she had in the backseat and turned up the music. By the time we got to the theater a few minutes later I was feeling nice.

"Whose turn is it to pick the movie?" I asked as I hopped out the car.

"I don't know." Summer said. "Let's go find out."

We all met up in the lobby to look over our choices. There were about four movies on the board that we all wanted to see.

"Who's choosing?" Emerald asked.

"Well, technically it's my turn," Gainell started, "but since this is Wren's night, I think she should pick the movie."

"Girl I don't care what we see. Let's just get in there."

"What about *Between Two Friends*?" Emerald suggested.

Phoenix rolled her eyes, but I'm probably the only one that caught it.

"What's that about?" Giuseppina asked.

"It's about two friends who find out they've been sharing each other's lovers. It seemed interesting in the previews I saw last week."

She glanced over at Phoenix, but for some reason I felt like it was a direct attack towards me.

"I think we should pick something else." Phoenix said.

"No, that sounds interesting." Wren backed up Emerald's suggestion. "That's what I want to go see. Let's watch someone else's drama for once. Who's with me?"

Everyone agreed to go see the movie. Phoenix and I were the only ones not really feeling it.

"I'm with Phoenix." I said. "I don't want to go see that."

"Why?" Wren asked. "Too close to home?"

My heart dropped into the pit of my stomach. I knew she was onto me. I was about to spill all my guts. Thank goodness she cut me off.

"Girl I'm just playing with you!" Wren laughed. "Come on, y'all. This is girl's night. We can't split up, and y'all know majority rules. Get your tickets so we can get our asses in there!"

The diva of the night has spoken. We all got our tickets and snacks from the concession stand and headed inside of the theater. Our seats were all the way at the top as always. We sat through at least twenty minutes of surveys, advertisements, and those goofy interviews they usually show before the previews. We were back to laughing and joking around with each other.

Then the lights went dim and the real previews began. After another ten minutes the movie started.

Whoever wrote this movie must have been following me around for the past four months. Every damn scene of the lead character, Kisha, was me. The only difference is that Wren wasn't sleeping with my man while I was sleeping with hers. This was strictly a one-way fuck over and I'm the one doing the fucking. I looked over to see Wren's reaction to the movie. Every time I looked down the row her face was expressionless. I couldn't read what she was thinking. Wren's always been the type to get drawn into a good story. There was no telling if she liked it or hated it until the end. This movie was barely two hours long, but it felt like we were in that theater forever.

When the credits began rolling and the lights came on most of us were shocked, appalled and in tears. The ending of the movie was so sad and lifelike. Not one of the couples survived their relationships; everything ended for everyone and they all went their separate ways. That was my biggest fear; that Wren would never be able to forgive me. I tried to keep it together, but I was feeling nauseous. Before the girls could figure out what was wrong with me, I headed straight for the restroom.

My entire dinner went down the toilet...literally. Every orifice of my body had something spewing from it. I felt like shit warmed over then sautéed and fed to the dirtiest, grimiest dog. Thank goodness it didn't all happen at the same time. After my episode was over I rinsed my mouth out and splashed water on my face. The smell in the bathroom was atrocious. I got out of there as soon as I could.

The girls met up with me in the lobby. I could finally get a sense of how Wren felt about the movie - and possibly how she would feel once I revealed my own secret.

"Damn, girl, you left us hanging!" Gainell said.

"I had to go really bad!" I covered it up with a laugh. "What did y'all think of the movie?"

Almost everyone started talking about how messed up it was, how it was a good movie, and what they would have done differently if they were one of the girls. Wren was the only one who didn't express an opinion. That almost made me sick all over again.

"What about you, Wren? I know you would have gone ham on them if that was you!"

I was hoping she would catch my humor behind the statement and not my confession.

"It was good. Deep, but it hit a little too close to home. Come on, girls. We have to be at Lollipop Land in fifteen minutes before we lose our reservation."

I'm fucked!

We all headed back to our cars and followed each other to the highway. My stomach was so queasy that I didn't want anything else to drink. The secret was bound to come out sooner or later. Guilt was literally eating me alive from the inside out. I really fucked up this time.

"Summer, I'm pregnant."

Summer jerked the car over three lanes and slammed on the breaks. She almost caused a pile-up behind us. With the car on the shoulder and us out of harm's way I broke down once again.

"How? Wait. Laila, please tell me Jason is not the father."

I was silent.

"Laila!" She screamed at me. "Don't fuck with me! Tell me that you are not about to fuck up this entire group by having Jason's baby!"

I've never seen Summer get this angry before. At that moment, I feared her more than Wren.

"I can't. I don't know who the father is."

"I thought it was just one time, Laila! How in the hell are you pregnant by Jason if you just fucked him one time?"

I couldn't look her in the eye and tell her Jason and I had been creeping around for three months. It was bad enough I couldn't guarantee he was the father. It would be worse once Wren found out. At this point I was ready for the secret to be out and this entire night to be over. The problem was I wasn't ready to tell it. Not yet.

"Alright, Laila! Enough is enough. This shit is going to get told tonight and you're going to tell it. There is no way you're dragging me down with you. Enough of the games, Laila. It's time to woman up and face your mistake."

"I can't tell her, Summer. She's going to kill me."

"You can tell her, and you will tell her. If you don't then she'll kill both of us. I love you, but I'm not dying for your sin."

"Bitch please, don't you dare start throwing around the sin word. You're the biggest sinner I know!"

"Excuse you?"

"Summer, you don't do anything but sit around, moping, whining, and complaining about your life. You work all day and drink, smoke, and do God knows what else all night. You are so fucking lackadaisical it's ridiculous!"

"This isn't about me, alright! What I do in my life is my business!"

"What life, Summer? We've been trying to push you to get a life for years and you won't budge! Hell, I had to practically pull teeth to get you to come out tonight!"

"Since when is being lazy a sin?"

"Bitch read a bible for once! Everyone knows that laziness is a sin. It's called being a sloth…"

"…as opposed to being a slut?"

I sat back in my seat, slapped in the face by my own point. She was right. I had absolutely no reason to jump on her when I had my own mess to clean up. If ever there was a moment for me to be speechless this is one of them. Regardless of how hard I try to shine a light on someone else's skeletons, mine kept casting a shadow of their own. She knew it just as much as me.

"I'm sorry, Summer. You're right. I didn't mean to lash out on you like that."

"Yes, you did." She said. "You don't seem to understand that when you have a certain level of liquor in your system you tell the truth, the whole truth, and nothing but the truth. This is one of those moments. But I'm not mad at you because you're right. I have been a sloth for the past few years. You all have tried to help me, but I refused it. Maybe I do need help. In fact, I know I do. One of these days I will get it, but right now we're not talking about me. You are the one that has some demons to face. Mine will be dealt with at an appropriate time. Yours, however, must be addressed now."

"But I don't want to lose her."

I leaned over and broke down in tears on her lap.

"I know, sweetie, but that's not your decision to make. After the pole dancing class, you need to tell her. Don't think, just act. Remember, no matter what happens between you two I will always be here for you."

"Even after I just cursed you out?"

"I can't get mad at you for telling the truth. I know my demons, Laila. I deal with them every day. I own up to my sin. It's time for you to own up to yours."

I sat up in my seat and she wiped the tears away from my eyes.

"You're right. It must be done tonight. Besides, I'm not keeping this baby. You won't find me on four episodes of Maury!"

"Four? Really, Laila?!" Summer said in disgust.

"I know, it's horrible. I'm horrible. Let me get over this hump first. I can't handle more than one sin at a time."

"Let's go. If we take too long, they'll start blowing us up."

Just as she said that her phone began to ring. It was Gainell.

"We got caught up behind an accident and had to jump off. We'll be there in a minute."

"Are you two okay?" I heard her say through the phone.

Summer looked over at me and grabbed my hand.

"We'll be fine. See y'all in a minute." I hung up the phone. "Thanks, Summer."

"You're welcome. And you owe me a bottle for every time you called me a bitch."

"I'm not adding to your addiction!"

"Until I address my issues, oh yes the hell you are!"

We slipped back into traffic and got off two exits early. Within two minutes we were at Lollipop Land. When we walked in everyone's face was shocked. What we saw on the screen blew us away. I may be saved after all.

Phoenix

Everyone's eyes were on me and I don't mean directly. How in the hell did this happen? My entire body was sprawled across the projector screen; flashes of scenes with me and random lovers from my past. It was bad enough that my girls were witnessing this, but there were a bunch of random chicks in the room, too. They were gasping and pointing, a couple of them reacted as if it was their man in the picture. This was embarrassing…this was horrifying…this had Emerald's name written all over it.

The tape cut off just as we heard the moaning of a woman. It didn't sound like me, but after what was just displayed, I wasn't willing to take any more chances. I sat in the middle of these women feeling so vulnerable and exposed. Every emotion in me activated and I could no longer control myself. I looked over at Emerald with tear filled eyes. She sat there with the biggest grin on her face. If anyone took pleasure in humiliating me, it was her.

"Well, my job here is done." She said with a snide tone. "You ladies have a great night."

She stood up and reached down to grab her workout bag from the floor. Turning her back on me was the worst mistake she made in her life. I grabbed the first think I could feel in my purse which was my taser. In one swift motion I tackled her and shocked the shit out of her. The Taser was strategically placed between her legs. She was poised to have the world's biggest and most painful camel toe in history.

"Get off me!"

Those were her last words before I sent 50,000 volts of pure, uninterrupted electricity straight through her vagina. Everyone in the room tried to pull me off her, but I was not letting go until she was no longer moving. That didn't take long seeing as this Taser is extremely powerful. Once I felt she was out for the count I got off her, but not before spewing a few venomous words at her.

"You lifeless sorry ass bitch! How dare you think you can get away with exploiting me? What the fuck have you been smoking, you senseless hoe? Did you really think I was going to buckle under your attack? Did you?"

She didn't answer, so I kicked her right in the vagina.

"Bitch I own you! I made you! You are nothing without me and don't you ever fucking forget that!"

I hacked up the biggest, thickest, nastiest spit wad I could and aimed it straight at her mouth. She was still paralyzed from the taser and couldn't move.

"Phoenix!" Gainell rushed over and pushed me against the wall, knocking me back into reality. "What the fuck is wrong with you!? You can't just go around tazing people like that! You two may be beefing right now, but deep down inside you know she's still your friend and it's killing you that you two aren't speaking right now."

"Nelli, are you off your fucking rocker?" I was ready to explode all over again. "What kind of fucking friend exploits someone by posting a series of sex scenes set to stripper music? Don't you dare try to stand there and defend that lame bitch! She got exactly what she deserved, and she better be glad the taser was the first thing I grabbed!"

"Listen, Phoenix," Laila said, standing between Gainell and me, "yes she fucked you over, but there are worse things she could have done to you. I'm not saying what she did was right, but now you're just as guilty as she is."

"Blah, blah, mother fucking blah! You bitches just don't get it. My pride is the only fucking thing I have in this world and she's trying to destroy it!" I pointed down at her still body. "There is no way in hell I'm going to let that lowlife, classless bitch ruin that for me!"

"It's not that damn serious, Phoenix!" Laila screamed.

"How in the hell would you know, Laila? You live for sucking and fucking dicks! That's your M.O. right?"

"Whoa!" Giuseppina intervened. "Now you're getting personal, Phoenix. Laila is just trying to help you."

"How in the hell is she trying to help me? If anything, she's defending that bitch down there! Take your Italian sausage looking ass on somewhere! Go have a burger or something, you fat bitch!"

Slap!

Did Gainell just hit me? That bitch has officially lost her mind.

"Don't you ever talk to my sister like that, do you understand me?"

"I'll talk to whomever I want however I want."

"The hell you will. Let something else come out your mouth sideways at her again and those will be the last words you'll say."

"What are you going to do? Put a hit out on me? Oh, I forgot, that's what you mobster mother fuckers are known to do. I'm sure you got the money for it. Why do you care anyway? I'll toss you a stack and you'll forget that you even have a sister."

"Phoenix you're out of control." Summer said, trying to intervene.

By now the director has made her way downstairs and threatened to put us all out. The other women in the room were sitting and watching as if this was a reality TV show. I was tired of my pride being attacked. It was time to put all these bitches on blast.

"Don't fucking stand there and tell me that I'm out of control you drug addict. Every single one of you got your own skeletons to deal with. Summer, you're the laziest bitch I've ever met! Nellie you're the most materialistic, but I guess you need to be when you don't know shit! GiGi is one footlong away from a damn heart attack."

"Phoenix calm down!" Laila said. "You're going to do something that you'll regret.

"I already have. I let this bitch invade my space."

"Okay, so maybe she went over the top…" Laila began.

"Maybe?!"

"Okay, she did go over the top. That's no reason to be violent towards her. There are other ways to handle this, Phoenix. She could have done much worse."

"Laila, that bitch attacked the one thing she knew was the most important to me! How in the hell could this get any worse?"

"At least she didn't get pregnant by your man." Summer blurted out.

The look on Laila's face dropped. She lost all color in her skin at that very moment. Any ounce of anger I felt at that moment was sucked in by Wren. She looked up at Laila like she was ready to rip her head off.

"Say that again?" Wren said in the calmest voice.

"Summer!" Laila screamed. "How could you?"

"No, Laila." Wren said. "How could you?"

Without saying another word Wren got her coat and purse and walked up the stairs to leave.

"Wren, wait!"

Laila ran up the stairs after Wren.

"Thanks a lot, Phoenix! You've officially fucked up our night." Gainell said.

She also went to chase after Wren along with Summer and Giuseppina. Once again, all eyes were on me. I started to calm down and began to feel bad. This was some complete and utter bullshit.

"Fuck!"

I went to go after the girls. I owed every single one of them an apology. Emerald was finally able to start moving, albeit very slow. Tears flooded my eyes as I accepted the fact that Gainell was right. It was killing me what she did. I honestly thought we were better than that. Even though we weren't friends I never in a million years thought she would be that vindictive. I expected retaliation, but not like this.

"I hope it was worth it." I said, looking down on her.

She let out a moan as she tried to get up. Everything in me wanted to kick her again, but what would that solve? Right now, I had five other friends outside that I needed to make up with. This one can stay on the ground and fend for herself. I stepped over her and made my way up the stairs.

Wren

My whole world collapsed around me. I knew there was something going on between Jason and Laila. I never expected one of my own best friends to betray me that way. The pain I'm feeling right now is indescribable. My heart hurt so badly; I wanted to rip it out so I wouldn't have to feel it beat. There were so many angry voices in my head. It was hard to hear them because they were all yelling and screaming at the same time. He was my life, my world; I was willing to die for him. How could he kill me like this? How could she help him?

I sat in my car with the door wide open and the engine running. This was the last place I wanted to be. Every part of me wanted to run away and not look back; go start a new life somewhere else and forget the fact that tonight ever happened. I reached in the glove compartment and pulled out my 9MM. In one sentence I lost my man, my best friend, and everything that I thought was right with my life. Why should I go on? Everything was so heavy. My arms dropped between the seats. The only thing I had the strength to do was cry.

And then I heard her voice.

"Wren, please listen to me!" I heard Laila screaming as she ran up to my car. "I'm so sorry! I didn't mean for any of this to happen. You know I love you like a sister and would never intentionally hurt you. Please, Wren, forgive me. You don't have to speak to me if you don't want, but please say you forgive me! Please!"

I sat in my car rocking back and forth. The tears were still flowing but I was no longer sobbing. The voices in my head began to get loud again. I didn't know what to do. The pain intensified with every word I heard her speak. This was not going to end well.

Laila

My words were falling on deaf ears. Wren didn't want to hear anything I had to say, but I needed her to listen to me. I begged and pleaded for her forgiveness while everyone stood back and looked on. There was so much adrenaline in the air that I no longer cared how bad I looked. I was wrong and I admitted it. If losing Wren as a friend was my punishment then I was willing to accept my fate, but not before I expressed myself.

"You don't ever have to speak to me again, but I want you to know that I'm so sorry, Wren. I'm not even keeping the baby. I can't even guarantee that it's his baby. Nothing has to change between you and Jason. I promise to never cross that line again. I'm already being punished by losing my child. I don't want to lose you, too."

I began to break down. She wasn't saying a word, but I needed that closure. I leaned in to give her a hug. Not to make me feel better, but to show her I was being genuine.

"I'm sorry, Wren. I'm so sorry!"

I felt her arm come up around my shoulder. She began to squeeze me tightly. I started to cry harder. She was hugging me back. Maybe there was hope after all. I buried my head in the side of her neck and began to cry harder. She raised her other arm and I felt a soft pop. There was pressure in my belly that started to cramp badly.

"I'm sorry! I'm so sorry! I'm so…"

Those were my last words before she pushed me off her and I fell back in the parking lot. There were screams coming from the building.

"Oh my God! Somebody call 911!"

That soft pop was a gun shot. Wren had put one right in my uterus. She closed her door and sped off before anyone could get to me. This was the fate that I deserved. I should have never crossed that line with her fiancé. Now I was paying the price. There was so much panic around me. Everyone was crying, lights were flashing, yet I wasn't a part of any of it. It felt like I was hovering over everyone, watching the scene from a distance. Little did I know, when the doors shut to the ambulance that would be the last time my friends would see me alive.

Fuggi il piacere presente, che accenna dolor futuro. - Skip the enjoyment that you will regret.

Wren

...and that's how I got here. The entire neighborhood was on lockdown. They cut the power to all the houses in the area. All because this mother fucker decided to fuck my best friend and give her a baby, my baby! I stared at his lifeless body lying across what used to be our bed. Our crisp white linen was covered with fragments of his brain. He never saw it coming. I didn't want to give him the opportunity to try and talk me out of it. And the bitch on the floor? Well, she was just in the wrong place at the wrong time.

How did my life come to this? What did I do to deserve to be treated so cruelly? He's the one that cheated on me and I'm the one they're trying to negotiate with? This shit is not fair! He should be the one to pay for his sins, not me! I didn't do anything wrong. I loved him unconditionally. I cooked for him, cleaned for him, supported and encouraged him. Even when he was caught cheating, I forgave him! I forgave him time and time again, and this is how he repays me? By fucking one of my ex-best friends for months and then getting her pregnant as if I was never going to fucking find out?!

Why do they keep flashing those damn lights in my window? The stupid phone keeps ringing and they keep yelling at me through that bullhorn. They're causing a scene and I want them all to leave me the fuck alone.

"GO AWAY!!!" I start screaming at the top of my lungs. "ALL OF YOU JUST GO AWAY!!!"

I began to throw anything I could get my hands on. Vases, glasses, and figurines all splattered against the wall of my bedroom. I broke so many things that glass covered my bedroom floor. The anger brought me down to my knees and I started crying uncontrollably. I begged God to take this pain away from me. Why was I paying for his mistakes? I looked across the room and saw a frame with our most recent picture. I stepped around the bed and over this lifeless young lady's body and picked it up.

It felt hot and heavy. Nothing in the picture made sense. In my place was the image of a woman that I no longer recognized, even though I knew it was me. In his place was the devil; a demon looking figure that had lies and deceit buried deep down in their soul.

"YOU FUCKING LIAR!"

I took the frame and threw it at his head. Repeatedly I beat him with it until his face was unrecognizable. When the frame broke, I grabbed the phone and continued to beat on his body for what seemed like hours. Something had come over me; an evil I had never encountered before. When it got tired of beating on him it turned on me.

"I HATE YOU! I HATE YOU! I HATE YOU!" I screamed over and over as I threw myself all over the room. The glass and shattered fragments on the floor were cutting away at my body as I crashed, crawled, and rolled all over the room.

"HOW COULD YOU DO THIS TO ME?!"

The voices were now verbal, loud, and angry. I cried and cried until my eyes were sore. Every tear felt like acid running down my cheek. It burned me to the core. I felt like scratching my eyes out. They hurt so much. The pain was unbearable. I lost everything. There was no reason for me to go on.

Please make it stop.

I heard a small voice inside of me say this over all the anger and hostility. Everyone else went out with a bullet. I needed to feel this pain leave my body for good. If I made it feel even half as bad as it made me feel it would go away. The knife slid through my jugular like a hot knife through butter. Suddenly, the pain started to release from me. The voices became quieter until there was nothing left but silence, calm, and peace.

Che gli dei vogliono distruggere in primo luogo fanno impazzire. - Whom the gods wish to destroy, they first make mad.

The Aftermath

Summer

They're gone. They're both gone and it's my fault. That's been my centering thought since Laila died and they found Wren's body in her home. If only I had kept my mouth shut, they would both still be here. Maybe not talking to each other, but they'd still be here. There isn't much to life sitting in a padded room. My nerves couldn't handle losing someone I loved in such a gruesome way. It was safer in here for me. I didn't have to worry about bills, I got free food and medication, and I will never have to worry about anyone accusing me of ruining their life again. The asylum isn't so bad. I could spend the rest of my life here. Rocking back and forth I attempted to make myself believe that lie. Maybe I will one of these days.

Con nulla non si fa nulla. - From nothing, nothing came.

Emerald

No one has called to speak to me since the night Laila and Wren died. They all think it's my fault as if I'm the one that coerced Laila to sleep with Wren's man. It's just as well; I never fit in with that group anyway. If anything, they owe me an apology, especially Phoenix. It's because of her that I can no longer have children. Between her taser and kicking me she destroyed my uterus and my chances of having a baby are less than ten percent. Not only has she turned everyone against me, but she ruined any chances of me having a child. Something else I can't have, thanks to her. One of these days she's going to pay majorly for what she's done to me. I won't say when, where, or how, but when it happens she'll wish she was dead.

Il piu povero che sia in terra è l'avaro. - The covetous man is good to none and worse to himself.

Phoenix

Thanks to the owner of Lollipop Land and Emerald I'm now on probation for three years. Do you know what it feels like to be watched like a hawk? I'm required to do check-ins, random drug tests, and attend this anger management class. All because she wanted to get revenge since I wouldn't talk to her anymore. What kind of silly shit is that? Well there was nothing I could do about it now. At least I don't have to deal with her crazy ass anymore. She's such a spiteful bitch. If it wasn't for her, I'd still have my freedom, the girls would still all get along, and Laila and Wren would still be here. That last part hurts me the most. One day I'll be free from all of this, but no matter what happens I'll never get my best friends back. That's one thing I will never forgive her for. Never.

La superbia viene davanti alla rovina. - Pride comes before the fall.

Giuseppina

After Wren and Laila's funerals I went with my sister and mother back to Italy. My heart was so heavy because I loved them both so dearly. None of this had to happen in my opinion, but it did. Gainell and I lost every single friend we had that night. Wren and Laila died, Phoenix went to jail, Summer had a mental meltdown, and Emerald - well, fuck her. Our once unbreakable bond shattered into a million pieces, with some never being recovered again. I found my comfort in food, going from 180 pounds to 250 pounds in a month. Gainell never said a word, but she was grieving in her own way. It is safe to say that my life will never be the same.

Ne uccide più la gola che la spada. - Gluttony kills more than the sword.

Gainell

After the funerals and once I touched down in Italy, I became the ostrich in the sand and buried myself in work. From the second my eyes opened until they closed while in the middle of a project, I kept myself busy. I couldn't stand seeing everything fall apart around me. I lost my two best friends permanently in a way that would make anyone scream. Phoenix's incarceration made me hate Emerald for life. Summer went bonkers on us. GiGi, my sweet sister, is on the verge of having a massive heart attack. What's even worse is that none of this can be fixed with money. I couldn't buy my friend's lives back. I couldn't pay for Phoenix's freedom, although I did pay for her attorney. I can't purchase stock in sanity to save Summer. I did put a hit out on Emerald though. She'll get what's coming to her in due time. If Phoenix wasn't right about anything else, she was spot on about me hiring a hit woman. After everything that's happened, I feel it's safe to say that there is truth in the saying, "If you live by the sword, you die by the sword."

Chi due lepri caccia, l'una non piglia e l'altra lasciata. - Grasp all, lose all.

About the Author

"Writing is not only my passion; it's my purpose." That is evident in every novel, short story, article, and literary work produced by Diamond Cartel. Since the age of eight, writing has been a way for her to express what she's feeling, thinking, and experiencing in life. With several novels, compilations, and motivational books under her belt, Diamond utilizes her passion for words to tell a story to the hearts, minds, and spirits of her readers. Adding her own twist to traditional storytelling, Diamond doesn't just write to entertain, but also to empower and encourage. That is why she is the self-professed "novelist like no other."

Outside her role as a novelist, Diamond also doubles as coach and Self Love Advocate. Under this persona, her goal is to motivate, inspire, and teach others the fundamentals of being successful and following your passion while fully loving yourself in the process. Diamond believes everyone has a gift within them. She uses this insight to help you gain clarity, create a plan of action, and provide you with the tools you need to progress along your path.

After all I said and done, Diamond loves to simply live and experience life. As an avid explorer, she loves to travel. No distance is too great or too small for exploring. She also loves to spend quality time with her children, get lost in a night of music and dancing, and make others laugh like there's no tomorrow. Diamond truly lives to love and loves to live.

For more information on products and services offered by Diamond and ISYS please visit www.isysconnections.com.

Made in the USA
Columbia, SC
07 July 2019